PICK
POCKET

A NOVEL

JUDITH BLEVINS &
CARROLL MULTZ

PICKPOCKET

COPYRIGHT © 2019
BY JUDITH BLEVINS
& CARROLL MULTZ

PUBLISHED BY

ShahrazaD Publishing®

Library of Congress Control Number:2019909197

ISBN - 978-1-64633-603-6

CONTACT THE AUTHORS AT:

judyblevins@bresnan.net

carrollmultz@charter.net

ALSO BY THE AUTHORS

Novels

By Judith Blevins

Double Jeopardy • *Swan Song*
The Legacy • *Karma* • *Paragon*

By Carroll Multz

Justice Denied • *Deadly Deception*
License to Convict • *The Devil's Scribe*
The Chameleon • *Shades of Innocence*
The Winning Ticket

By Judith Blevins & Carroll Multz

Rogue Justice • *The Plagiarist* • *A Desperate Plea*
Spiderweb • *The Méjico Connection* • *Eyewitness*
Lust for Revenge • *Kamanda* • *Bloodline*

Childhood Legends Series®

By Judith Blevins & Carroll Multz

Operation Cat Tale • *One Frightful Day*
Blue • *The Ghost of Bradbury Mansion*
White Out • *Flash of Red*
Back in Time • *Treasure Seekers*
Summer Vacation-Part 1:
Castaways-Part 2: Blast Off

CONTENTS

A NOTE FROM THE AUTHORS

Sometimes life's journey leads us in unintended directions. Venturing forward often without even a clue as to where we will end up is what makes life interesting. It's also inevitable that not all decisions we make along the way will be valid ones. Sometimes we are in control of our destinies and other times our destinies have already been mapped out for us.

In *Pickpocket*, our protagonist is placed in a precarious situation—one that is not of her doing but one nevertheless that requires the genius of Einstein, the patience of Job and the protection of one-thousand guardian angles. Even then, everything hinges on the luck of the draw.

Placing insurmountable obstacles in the path of the good guys is easy for the writer. Providing them with parachutes in building believable plots is not. In real life there are no magic wands to waive nor are there in the novel you are about to read. Exonerating the innocent and convicting the guilty is and will always be the goal of your authors. Hopefully, that is and will always be the goal of our readers.

Special thinks to those who have contributed to making *Pickpocket* a novel to remember: Margie Vollmer Rabdau, Lisa Knudsen, and last but not least, to Frank Addington, our book designer.

DEDICATION

To those who stand firm
on ethical principles
despite the temptations.

*No one
ever
suddenly
became
depraved.*

Juvenal

PROLOGUE

"What do you mean you don't have it!" Ricco demands.

Tony is visibly shaken; you can hear it in his voice "Like I said, boss, I had it here one minute," Tony pats his jacket pocket, "and it's gone the next..."

"Yeah! Gone? Gone where?"

"Donno. When I left the mall, I went to my ride and drove straight here—no stops along the way."

"Un-huh!" Rubbing his face with his hands, Ricco eventually looks up and asks, "Did anything unusual happen between the mall and the parking lot?"

"Nope!" Tony answers. Then after a brief pause, he adds, "Well, not unless you call bumping into one of those freaky female teens who hang out there unusual."

It takes a moment for Ricco to connect the dots. He then slaps his forehead with the palm of his hand "You dim-wit!" he shouts. "Damn little bitch picked your pocket."

Tony looks stunned for a moment, then replies, "Naw! Couldn't of...I'd of known..."

Ricco furrows his brow. "Yeah, sure! You wouldn't know if you'd been run down by a Mack truck. Good thing I had our client put a tracking device in the package…"

"What! Tracking device!" Tony blurts, his voice dripping with righteous indignation. "Why you… you… Don't you trust me?"

"Don't trust anyone with ten thousand dollars—especially fools like you. And it's not just the dough. That was a down-payment on the contract. The package also contained instructions which could be disastrous if they fall into the wrong hands. We gotta get that package back pronto or we're all dead. Now get your ass outta here and retrace your steps. Don't come back until you've retrieved the package."

"But…"

"No buts! It'll be yours if you don't find it and mine as well."

CHAPTER ONE

Button, Button, Who's Got The Button...

M y name is Megan Duval. Jessica Stanton and I were roommates at Wellington-York University in D.C. all four of our undergraduate years. During those lean years, my only means of survival were my scholarship and student loans—and even as frugal as I was, I barely skimped by. Jess, on the other hand, was always rolling in dough. I marveled at her ability to extend her finances. She ate out often, always had new clothes, and the latest cellphone and computer technology. This puzzled me because, as far as I knew, she didn't have family or other support outside of her scholarship and student loans. I remember the day I asked her how she multiplied the loaves and fishes and managed to have so much spending money.

Without flinching or even looking up from the book she was studying, she replied, "Elementary, my dear Watson. I pick pockets."

Thinking she was joking, I tossed a paperclip at her and teased, "Sure ya do."

Unabashed, Jess set her textbook aside. Looking up at me, she reiterated, "No, really, Meg. I'm a pickpocket—and a pretty damn good one at that. I learned the craft from my cellmate during a stint in juvenile detention. You know how those places stress the importance of learning a trade. Well…," she smiled, "I did. One that would keep me financially independent."

I shook my head in disbelief. I guess the look on my face urged her to offer proof of her admission. "Okay, then, Doubting Thomas, let me show you." She plucked a small notepad from her desktop and handed it to me. It was about the size of a man's wallet. She then said, "Step out into the corridor and put the notepad into any one of your pockets. When you're ready just walk into the room the way you normally would."

Even though I remained skeptical, I took the notepad from her. Not wanting to be the butt-end of a joke, I examined the notepad for telltale signs of deception. When I was satisfied it was what it purported to be, I agreed to the demonstration and left the room closing the door behind me. Out in the corridor, I put the notepad in my front jeans pocket. It was a tight fit and I reasoned there was no way she could extract it without my knowing it. Confident I had outsmarted her, I opened the door and announced, "Ready or not, here I come."

Jess barely took notice when I reentered the room. Thinking I was pretty clever, I sashayed past her desk. When I did so she slowly stood, and turning my direction, she ever so slightly bumped me. Before I could take another step she tapped me on the shoulder and handed me the notepad.

Stunned, I exclaimed, "No way!" I immediately slipped my hand into my jeans pocket—it was now empty, the notepad was gone. "How'd you do that?" I asked, baffled by the ease with which she picked my pocket.

With a smug expression, Jess asked, "Now, are you convinced?"

In our spare time over the next few weeks, Jess patiently taught me the time-honored art of pickpocketing. That was over five years ago. Although I never used my new found talent in real life, I suspected Jess continued to supplement her income by a profession that went back to biblical times and maybe even further.

● ● ●

When we completed our education, we both secured good jobs. Jess' degree in journalism, along with her petite figure, exotic good looks, and effervescent personality were assets that were probably too hard for a potential employer to resist. She was hired as a copywriter by a local D.C. non-bias weekly publication, *The Washington Witness.*

My degree in political science landed me a job with the CIA doing research in the international relations division. Having been influenced by the glitz and glamour of Hollywood's version of espionage, my goal was to eventually become a field agent. Jess often teased me, "Honey, with what you've got goin' for you, you could audition for the next Bond girl."

• • •

Jess and I bonded during our college years and were as close as sisters. Staying in touch was important to us so we arranged a standing luncheon date. We'd meet weekly at the Downtown Deli on DuPont Circle in D.C. The deli was situated a few blocks from Jess' workplace and only ten miles from CIA headquarters. The hour whizzed by as we eagerly shared our week's adventures. It was during the most recent of those luncheons that Jess told me about striking the mother lode.

"Meg, you're not going to believe this but…," Jess began but stops midsentence and glances around the deli.

I follow her gaze but don't detect anything unusual. "But what?" I urge, perturbed by the melodrama and impatiently look at my watch.

Jess reaches across the table and grabs my hand in a tight grip. I feel her tremble and it's then I realize she's troubled about something, seriously troubled.

"What is it, Jess?" I ask.

Extracting her hand from mine, she says, "I lifted a bundle yesterday. Haven't counted it yet but it must be at least a ten or even twenty thou."

Stunned, but not totally believing her, I drop my fork onto my plate and stare at her. "Come on—"

"No, really." Jess anxiously looks around again before continuing. "I was hanging out on the mezzanine at the mall looking for a target, you know, an easy mark. That's when I spotted two guys dressed in business suits seated at one of the tables in café court."

"Un-huh, then what?" I ask, still not sure Jess isn't pulling my chain.

"Well, Meg, how often do you see Armanis in café court? The way these dudes were dressed is what attracted my attention in the first place. I continued to watch them from my perch." Jess begins to shred her paper napkin as she continues her story. "They had their heads together engaged in serious conversation. After a few minutes, one of them rose and passed an envelope to the other. The envelope was the size of a stack of bills —

and bulging."

This cloak and dagger routine was unnerving me and time was fleeting. Looking at my watch again, I shift in my chair. If this is some kind of joke, I'm anxious for the punch line so I can get back to work.

Apparently noticing my discomfort, Jess rushes on. "I couldn't help myself, Meg. I had to know what was in the envelope and why their encounter was so clandestine. When they parted, they went different directions. I stalked the one with the envelope. As soon as the opportunity presented itself, I lifted it." Jess looks around again.

"Jess!"

"I know, I know!" she says. She picks up her glass and her hand shakes sloshing water out onto the table. She immediately sets the glass down. "But like I said," she exclaims, as we sop up the water with napkins, "I just couldn't help it."

A waitress appears and helps with the cleanup. I thank her and when she retreats, I ask Jess, "Where's the envelope now?"

"At my place. I went straight home from the mall. When I got there, I looked inside. There was so much money, I got scared and didn't take time to count it."

I rub my temples trying to think of a solution to

Jess' dilemma. "Well," I say, "you can't turn it over to the authorities, they'd arrest you."

"I realize that!" Jess snaps back at me. She immediately apologizes. "Sorry, Meg. I'm just a mess."

I nod, indicating I understand. Fidgeting with her now damp napkin, she asks, "Do you think you could hypothetically get advice from your boyfriend at the agency?"

I cringe at Jess' reference to Steve Cunningham, a senior CIA agent, as my boyfriend. I was assigned as his assistant when I first started with the CIA. With him having to be gone so much, he needed someone in the office he could rely on to research issues at a moment's notice and keep his itinerary. I guess in the private sector I'd be identified as his personal secretary.

I'm eager to dispel the notion that I'm romantically involved with Steve, so I jump to the defense. "For starters, he's not my boyfriend! We've had a few dates but nothing serious. Besides, he's in the field most of the time."

"Okay. Whatever!" Jess says, apparently wanting to avoid an argument. Then, sounding desperate, she adds, "Would you talk to him anyway?"

My better judgment tells me not to get involved in Jess' problem, much less involve Steve. Even hypothetically it would be embarrassing to ask his advice on such a matter. However, Jess is my best friend so I agree to help her if I can. My dilemma is that I don't want to implicate Jess or myself in anything illegal that could cost us our jobs. I cringe just thinking of how I could approach Steve without looking like a fool. And it occurs to me that my being a CIA employee, even knowing about a crime and not reporting it could have devastating effects on my career.

• • •

That evening, I agonize over how to best initiate the conversation with Steve. *Oh, by the way, Steve, just suppose I had a friend that picked some dude's pocket, and just suppose because of the contents of the grab, she needs advice on what to do with it…* I'm interrupted in the midst of my musings when I receive a frantic phone call from Jess.

"Meg, I'm in tru…trouble," she stammers. "Need help. Please, meet me at my place as soon as you can…"

Oh, no! I knew it… Before I can reply she disconnects. I gaze at my phone in disbelief. Jess is usually cool, calm and collected. Her frantic demeanor is totally out of character and my instincts are on full alert.

Fearing for Jess' safety, I rush to her apartment.

Her place isn't in the high rent district but it isn't in the slums either. The doorman recognizes me when I enter the lobby and waives me through. Taking the elevator to the third floor, I approach her apartment with care. Not knowing what to expect, I'm surprised to find her door slightly ajar. I gently nudge it open with my foot and carefully peer inside. The room is much too dark and much too quiet. The hair at the back of my neck tingles as I reluctantly step inside quietly closing the door behind me. I want to call out to Jess but my instincts caution me to remain silent.

Pressing myself against the closed door, I stand motionless waiting for my eyes to adjust to the darkness. I detect the pungent odor of cigarette smoke in the apartment which alarms me. Jess abhorred smoking and wouldn't allow anyone to smoke near her. A few moments pass before I'm able to make out the interior of the room and I'm shocked at what I see. The room is in shambles. Contents of the desk drawers are strewn about; end tables are overturned; upholstery has been slashed; foam pulled from the cushions; and shattered lamps and broken glass desecrate the once tidy apartment.

What the hell?

Suddenly panic grips me. Trembling with fear, I break out in a cold sweat and my heart pounds wildly in my chest. *Has something dreadful happened to Jess?*

Against my better judgment, I move forward alert for movement from within. Nothing. As I continue slowly advancing toward her bedroom, I see what appears to be a pile of laundry lying on the floor in the hallway. *That's odd.* I creep closer and when I reach what I think is a bundle of laundry, I realize it's Jess. She's lying on her back. "Jess," I whisper and kneel beside her. I check for a pulse. There is none. I instinctively know Jess is dead.

My scream startles me into action. I place both hands on the floor to push myself up from the kneeling position. As I press my hands against the floor tiles, I encounter what feels like a knife lying next to the body. My rational self knows better, but my hysterical self picks up the knife. It's sticky to the touch, and realizing it's covered with blood, I immediately drop it. Stumbling out of the front door, I collapse in the corridor. I must have still been screaming because I soon find myself surrounded by a group of people emerging from the other apartments.

● ● ●

I find everything surreal. Some of the neighbors enter Jess' apartment, and upon discovering her lifeless body, one calls the police. Before long, the apartment complex is swarming with cops. Soon, an elderly woman urges me into her apartment away from the chaos. She helps me wash the blood from my hands. I'm shaking so violently, she wraps me in a crocheted shawl and makes me a cup of hot tea.

"Here, dearie," she says. "This'll make you feel better."

It tastes funny and I suspect it is laced with brandy. I down it in three gulps. That's where I am when I'm interviewed by Detective Chad Moran of the D.C. Metropolitan Police Department.

After taking my name, address and phone number, Moran began to quiz me about how I just happened to discover Jess' body. During my CIA induction, I learned to be truthful but not to volunteer any information. I kept my answers simple.

"Ms. Duval, do you usually visit your friends late at night?" Detective Moran asked.

"No."

"Then, how is it you were here tonight?"

"Jess called and asked me to come by."

"Hum. Did she say why?"

"No."

Moran looks puzzled and frowns. He finally asks, "Wasn't getting summoned by your friend in the middle of the night unusual?"

"Yes."

"And yet you didn't ask for details?"

"She disconnected before I had a chance."

"Uh-huh." Moran again frowns and flips a page on his notepad. "How long had you known the victim?"

"Nine years." When he says *victim* I fight to keep from completely breaking down.

"How did the two of you meet?" Moran asks in an authoritative voice, apparently unaware of my fragile condition.

I glance toward the door wishing I'd wake up and find this all was just a nightmare. "We were roommates at WYU," I answer.

"Un-huh," he says and scribbles something on his notepad. "Do you know if she has family?"

"None that I'm aware of."

"Do you know of anyone who would want to kill her?"

"No." Visions of our last luncheon jump into my mind, and remembering her confession, I wonder if her mark tracked her down. I squirm in my seat.

"Does she have a boyfriend?"

"Not that I'm aware of."

Moran rubs his forehead, apparently in exasperation. "You claim to be her best friend so how is it you know so little about her?"

"She was a very private person."

"I see," Moran says, with a hint of disbelief in his voice.

I cringe when I visualize Jess' lifeless body and want to bury my face in my hands to blot out the scene. *Poor Jess.*

Moran closes his notepad and stores it in his breast pocket. "That's enough for now. I'll have someone take you home. We'll continue the interview tomorrow at the station house—I'll send a car for you at nine."

I look up and say, "I have my car…"

"We prefer to escort you home—under the circumstances. You can pick up your car tomorrow after the interview."

Under the circumstances? Does he think I may be on the killer's list, too? I suddenly feel chilled, and not necessarily from the air conditioning.

• • •

Two uniformed officers escort me from the apartment building to their vehicle which is parked at the curb in front of the complex. The flashing lights are still on and I feel conspicuous. People are gathered on the sidewalk outside the apartment building, apparently wondering what's happening. One of the officers opens the backdoor for me, but before I get in, I glance over the top of the cruiser and notice a figure standing in a dark doorway across the street. He's smoking and the glow from the tip of his cigarette must be what attracted my attention. *Jess' killer?*

When we arrive at my place, the two officers accompany me inside. I wait nervously in the kitchen as they scour the premises making sure all the doors and windows are secure and no one is hiding in the closets or under the bed. After approximately ten minutes, they join me in the kitchen.

"Looks like you're safe enough," Officer Clancy says as he double checks the lock on the kitchen window.

I watch their every move and all of my senses are on overload. "Thank you," I manage to respond.

"Someone from the day shift will pick you up tomorrow morning," Clancy says, glancing around one more time. Apparently satisfied, he gestures to his partner and they prepare to leave. I walk them to the front door but before stepping out into the corridor, Clancy cautions me in a stern voice, "Don't let anyone in!" I nod, and as soon as they're clear, I double lock the door behind them.

Once I'm alone, dread encompasses me and the reality of Jess' murder begins to set in. I go into the living room and plop down on the edge of the sofa where, burying my face in my hands, I weep over the tragic loss of my friend. As I reach for the box of tissue I keep on the coffee table, I notice the pile of mail I picked up from my mailbox in the lobby when I came home from work. I remember just dumping the mail on the coffee table for later inspection. Sandwiched in between the usual collection of catalogs, flyers and bills is a manila envelope. *What the heck is this?* I pull it from the pile and examine the address. *Oh, my God. That's Jess' handwriting.* I instantly drop the envelope as if it were contaminated. *Is this what got Jess killed?*

My first thought is to call Detective Moran. However, I'm hesitant to do so remembering the interview. It felt as though I was a suspect. If this is what I think it is, the money could be construed as motive for murder and I probably wouldn't have a leg to stand on. I pick up the envelope and gently pry it open with my letter opener not worrying about disturbing any fingerprints on the outside. Since it was sent through the mail, no telling how many hands it had passed through before it got to me.

Emptying the contents out onto the coffee table, I gasp at what I see. There are multiple bundles of $100 dollar bills. I don't touch the contents, instead I rummage through my purse and find my makeup pouch. Using my eyebrow tweezers, I carefully count one of the bundles. It contains ten one-hundred dollar bills. Ten bundles would total ten thousand dollars. I remember today at lunch Jess remarked that she thought the envelope contained ten or twenty thousand dollars.

Sorting through the money with my letter opener, I find a smaller envelope sandwiched in between the scattered bundles—it isn't sealed. I carefully open the flap and pull a note from the smaller envelope with my tweezers. Even though my hands are shaking, I manage to unfold the note by using the letter opener and my tweezers. A dark, cold chill runs down my spine when I read:

> *Your target must be eliminated before the final Senate vote on Tuesday. If you screw this up, you may be the one in the crosshairs. You know how to contact me when the job is done.*

Oh, my God! Someone is marked for assassination. I need to talk to Steve!

CHAPTER TWO

Hide'n Seek...

I'm restless and pace the floor trying to decide what to do with the information I have in my possession. *Is the target a Senator? What bill is coming up for vote on Tuesday? Who could the assassin be and why?*

I'm suddenly now more terrified than ever. My nerves are on edge, and wringing my hands as I wallow in indecision, I pace back and forth through my home. As I pass my bedroom window, I carefully part the drapes and peer out into the night. *No! It can't be.* Standing in a doorway across from my apartment building I see the glow from the tip of a lit cigarette. *The killer must have followed the police cruiser to my place.* I immediately fall to my hands and knees, and crawling to the phone, I dial Steve's number. No answer. I don't call 911. I reason that my insisting upon having a person arrested for smoking while standing in a doorway across the street from my apartment would make me sound like an idiot. *Dammit!! Now the killer knows where I live I can't stay here but I don't have my car. Dammit! Dammit! Dammit!*

Staying low, I sit cross-legged on my bedroom

floor. That's when I notice my overnight case under the bed. I ease it out and open it up. I then crawl around my bedroom reaching up into drawers and tossing a few necessities into the small bag. Crawling into the living room dragging the suitcase behind me, I sandwich myself between the sofa and coffee table. I carefully put the bundles of money, including the note, back into the manila envelope and stash it in the suitcase on top of my clothes. Awkwardly duck-walking into the kitchen, I reach up and retrieve my iPhone, charger and purse from the countertop. As I cram my phone and charger into my purse, I notice my CIA ID badge attached to the shoulder strap and have an inspiration. *If I can make it to CIA headquarters alive, I can take refuge there until, until...* I don't waste time trying to figure out my next step.

Feeling somewhat better now that I have a plan, I use my iPhone and punch up the number for a taxi company. Must be a slow night, they answer on the first ring. I request a cab to pick me up at the rear entrance of my building and hope my nemesis doesn't have the back covered as well as the front. James Bond movies may be corny but I learned a few tricks from 007.

· · ·

Hunkering down, I pull my suitcase and purse through the living room to the front door and crack it open. Checking up and down the hallway, I conclude the coast is clear so I step out of my apartment. When I close the door behind me and hear the lock click into place, I suddenly feel exposed and vulnerable. I fight back the panic that threatens to overwhelm me. Taking deep breaths, I hurry down the fire stairs to the basement.

I'm heartened when I arrive without incident and push the heavy metal basement door open. Stepping inside, I maneuver my way through a maze of ducts, electrical panels and stored furniture as I make my way through the basement utility room. Carefully opening the building's rear entrance door, I slip out into the alley and press myself flat against the cool brick façade.

Even though the night air is chilly, I'm sweaty. My heart races and I'm having difficulty breathing. A sense of impending doom overwhelms me and my knees grow weak. I recognize these symptoms from my unstable childhood when I had panic attacks on a regular basis. I clinch my suitcase handle tightly and continue taking deep breaths to calm myself. Thankfully, a few minutes into my wait I see the cab round the corner into the alleyway and step out and flag it down.

The driver coasts to a stop next to where I'm standing and I literally jump into the backseat.

"Where to, lady?" the driver asks, as he engages the meter.

"CIA headquarters," I say, and turn to look out the rear window.

Looking back and apparently noticing my uneasiness, the driver asks, "Everything all right, lady?"

When I explain to him that I'm being stalked, he ignores the speed limit and we cover the ten miles to CIA Headquarters in record time. During the trek, I turn and hook my elbow over the back seat and keep watch out the window for any sign that we're being followed. I don't detect any tails. *Must've outsmarted 'em.*

When we approach the CIA building, I lean out of the passenger window and slide my keycard through the slot that opens the front gate. The cabbie blasts through the open gate and comes to a screeching halt at the front entrance. I toss some bills into the front seat, jump out and run up the steps. Before I slide my card through the slot at the entrance, I watch the cab driver blast through the still open front gate just before it closes. *God bless that man. He must've been a Nascar driver in his youth.*

Once inside, as I approach the metal detector, Jason, the night agent on duty recognizes me. "Ms. Duval, what brings you in so late?"

"Oh, ah…ah…I forgot to printout Mr. Cunningham's itinerary for tomorrow… Don't want him to miss an early meeting that was scheduled late today. I'll just print it out and leave it on his desk."

Since it was common knowledge that agent's assistants are allowed access to the agents' offices, Jason doesn't question me—or the suitcase I'm carrying.

"Roger that!" Jason replies and waves me through the metal detector.

• • •

Now that I'm inside the government building I'm feeling safer and more relaxed. Having gotten this far without being killed is reassuring. However, still trembling, my hands shake as I insert the key into the lock on Steve's office door. My plan is to lay low until Steve arrives. I'm confident he will know what to do.

Steve's office is dark and eerily quiet when I enter. The only illumination is a faint glow from the lights in the parking lot coming through the slats in the venetian blinds. Stepping inside, I place my suitcase against the wall next to the door. I'm familiar with the office and don't need to turn on the lights to find my way around. Exhausted, I curl up on the leather sofa and snuggle up under the navy blue throw, which is embroidered in gold and red with the CIA emblem. I finally feel that I'm now safe and protected. I didn't intend to fall asleep but the next thing I know I hear Steve talking on the telephone. His back is to me and he's looking out of one of the windows into the moonless night.

"...and you're supposed to be the professional!" he says in a loud voice.

By his tone, I can tell he's in a snit. I shrink back, cringing as I listen in stunned silence. I've never heard Steve lose his temper, at least not like this. I don't know what was said on the other end of the line but I hear Steve shout, "It's impossible that you could have traced it to this building. You better check your radar again, you incompetent idiot."

What's he talking about? Could Steve be involved in whatever it is that got Jess killed? My instincts tell me to remain quiet so I press back into the cushions. Since the room is dark, Steve apparently hadn't noticed me when he came in.

"Yes, you bumbling fool. Of course, I know her, she's my assistant." *He's talking about me!* I crunch lower into the sofa. After a pause Steve replies, "Call off your dumbass dog! I'll take care of it myself—

tonight!" He then violently slams down the phone and storms out the office banging the door closed behind him.

His words and tone of voice make it crystal clear that I'm the one slated to be taken care of—tonight! Adrenaline kicks in like never before and I take advantage of Steve's timely departure from the office. Jumping up from the sofa, I race across the room. Slinging my shoulder bag over my arm, I grab my suitcase, and cautiously crack the door open a few inches. When I do, I hear Jason's voice.

"...she went straight to your office as far as I know..."

"How long ago was that?" Steve demands in a loud, angry voice.

"Forty-five minutes or so..."

"Dammit!" Steve shouts, then adds, "Call extra security and get them over here ASAP!"

I don't wait for the rest of the conversation and make a mad dash further into the building away from the front entrance. I don't take time to try any of the doors; company protocol is to lock your office door when you leave. Now, as I race past the locked offices, my mind is whirling. *Where to hide? Where to hide? Where to hide?*

I'm close to being out of options when I see the restrooms at the end of the corridor. My instincts tell me to go into the men's room, not the women's. Panting from my sprint, I carefully ease the door open just wide enough for me to squeeze through and go to the furthest stall. Positioning my suitcase across the toilet seat, I ease myself onto it and pull my legs up against my chest. I nudge the door closed part-way and hug my knees with my arms. Unless Steve pushes the door open he won't be able to detect my presence. My heart is thumping a hundred miles an hour and my fight or flight instincts are battling it out. I want to keep on running but now there's nowhere to go. Common sense trumps my panic reflex and I scrunch up as small as I can and wait. When I hear the door to the men's room slam against the wall, I hold my breath. I know it's Steve. I listen as he rushes down the line of stalls banging the doors open as he goes. It's apparent he's in a rage.

I flinch as the stall doors make a hollow banging sound when he kicks them open one by one. "God damn, son-of-a-bitch…" he swears as he progresses in my location.

He's getting closer and I'm on the verge of trying to make a run for it although I know I'd never be able to get past him in the confined area of the men's room. I sit paralyzed waiting for Steve to discover me when I hear the main door to the men's room hit the wall as it's being slammed open. Apparently, Jason must have picked up on Steve's irritation and now he's slamming and banging doors around. When he enters, he interrupts Steve's quest.

"Mr. Cunningham," he shouts, "security has arrived…"

"About damn time," Steve sneers. Then his voice begins to fade as though he's moving away from me. "…have to do everything myself!" I hear him mutter, apparently walking toward Jason.

It suddenly gets very quiet and I'm guessing Steve left with Jason. I wait a few moments just to be sure and then move from my hiding place. When I was hired five years ago, I was given a tour of the building. Now, creeping down the corridor, I suddenly remember a fire exit on the lower level. The stairs are a few paces in front of me so I make a beeline for the exit. I hadn't been to the downstairs area since that initial tour and I'm hoping I can still find it. When I get to the bottom of the stairs, I see the red neon EXIT sign over the door at the far end. Wasting no time, I push through the fire door and almost jump out of my skin when an ear-splitting alarm begins to bellow. Now that my cover is blown, I run for dear life.

Racing around the outside of the building to the front, I spot a security vehicle parked at the main entrance. Apparently, the security guards Steve had Jason summon just converged on the building. They must have been in such a hurry they left the keys in the ignition with the motor running. *Manna from heaven. Thank you God!* I toss my suitcase in the backseat, slam the vehicle into gear and gun it straight for the front gate. I have a full head of steam and don't have the proclivity to stop even if I had enough driveway in front of me to do so. I push the petal to the metal and blast through the closed gates, ducking as sections of wrought iron assault the outside of the car and thump across the roof.

The windshield is shattered, however, I can still see where I'm going. The rearview mirror is useless and dangles at an odd angle on the shattered windshield. I take a quick look back over my shoulder. Steve and the security guards are standing on the front steps and Steve is waving his hands wildly in the air, apparently in exasperation. I swerve just in time to keep from hitting a light pole. Looking back could have cost me my life and I'm now too petrified to look back again. I just barrel through the late-night deserted streets headed for God knows where.

● ● ●

"Mr. Cunningham, how do you want us to proceed?" Aaron Drummond, one of the summoned secur_ty guards asks.

S_eve has apparently gone from angry to furious. "Which one of you imbeciles left the key in the ignition, for cryin' out loud!" Steve demands, then adds, "Never mind! Show me you can do something right and grab another car with a GPS and wait for further instructions."

Still raving at the lack of competence displayed by security, Steve storms back to his office. There, he places a call to Reggie Whitworth, the CIA IT specialist.

"Lo," Reggie answers, sleep evident in his voice.

"Reggie, Steve here. I need your immediate assistance. I'm at the office."

After a slight pause, Reggie says, "I'm on my way."

Steve spent the fifteen minute wait pacing the floor.

"I'm here, Steve," Reggie exclaims entering Steve's office. "What's the emergency?"

"Thank God! I need you to monitor the tracking device you gave me earlier this week."

"Sure, no problem. Let's go to the computer lab."

Once situated in front of a bank of computers, Reggie, after a few anxious minutes, honed in on the tracking device that was embedded in the manila envelope Meg had previously secured in her suitcase. The suitcase was now riding around in the backseat of the CIA vehicle she had commandeered.

"There it is," Reggie exclaims, tracing a moving light on the screen with his forefinger. The vehicle was traveling at a high rate of speed through the streets. Looking at the computer screen, Steve recognizes the map of the area and is able to pinpoint Meg's location. In the meantime, Agents Eric Watson and Kenneth Samuels, two of Steve Cunningham's top men show up and enter the computer lab.

"Thank God you're here," Steve says when they arrive. He points to the moving light on the computer screen, "This is the vehicle I want you to follow."

"Affirmative," Watson responds, "We're on our way and will probably intercept it within the hour. When we make contact, then what…"

"Bring the driver back here! And I want her alive."

"Roger that."

• • •

The adrenalin rush finally subsides and I'm feeling more secure since my getaway was successful. Luckily, traffic is light this time of night and I take the Arlington exit. Not having slept for over twenty-four hours, I can barely keep my eyes open. When I spot a Holiday Inn just off the highway, I decide to stop for a few hours.

The Holiday parking lot is pretty much filled up when I arrive. However, when I do find a slot and exit my vehicle, an elderly couple stops and examines the damage. "Ran into one hell of a hail storm coming across Kansas," I say. The couple whisper among themselves and move on. *Don't think they believe me—but who cares.*

I'm assigned an outside room on the second floor. Once settled in my room, I take a quick shower and put on a pair of jeans, a T-shirt, and the running shoes I packed when I fled home. I place the manila envelope next to my purse on the nightstand and pack my soiled clothes into the suitcase. Feeling safe, at least for the time being, I curl up on the queen sized bed fully clothed and am soon fast asleep.

The next thing I'm aware of is that it's full daylight. I must have been awakened by the noisy children screaming and laughing in the swimming pool on the ground level just outside my balcony. I turn over just in time to see silhouettes of two male figures pass by my window which faces the balcony. I'm now on full alert and out of bed in an instant. I go to the window and peek out through the slats in the vertical window shade. Although I can only see the backs of the two men who are slowly walking past the second story rooms, I recognize them. They're Watson and Samuels, two agents from the CIA!

Ducking back, I grab my purse and tuck the manila envelope under my arm. I take another quick look and see the agents are a few doors past my room. As I'm trying to decide if I can make a successful run for it, the door of the room next to mine opens and a portly woman steps out onto the balcony. I shrink back when she screeches at the children in the pool.

"You kids settle down! You're making too much noise. People are trying to sleep…"

I almost laugh at the irony of it. She was twice as loud as the kids. I watch Watson and Samuels whip around when they hear the commotion and start back my way. The irate mother is so large that her girth blocks their passage giving me time to run. I take the balcony stairs two at a time and head for the Holiday entrance. I didn't think my pursuers would try anything with other people around but who knows. When I approach the main entrance, I get another lucky break; the hotel shuttle is parked under the portico preparing to leave for the airport.

I join the throng of guests boarding the shuttle and take the seat right behind the driver.

The driver stores a clipboard in the console adjacent to the driver's seat. She puts the vehicle in gear, and looking back over her left shoulder apparently checking for traffic, she asks me, "What airline?"

"What...oh, ah, ah, Delta."

"Okay, miss. Delta is at the far end of the terminal and my last stop. Just stay on board and I'll get you there. Luggage?"

"Ah, no, no luggage." Thinking fast, I add, "It was lost and is still trying to catch up with me."

The driver nods. I keep my eyes glued to the window watching for suspicious cars.

• • •

Inside the terminal, I immediately rent a car and head back to D.C. I don't have a plan in mind, only that I need to find someone I can trust with the information I have. As I drive toward the capital, I ponder the note and wonder who the target could be and why. Tuesday is only two days away and I don't have a clue as to what to do.

• • •

Successfully making a getaway for the third or fourth time—I've lost count at this point—I wonder when my luck is going to run out. Like a cat, I hope

I have nine lives. My attention is distracted when my stomach growls and I realize I'm so hungry I could eat a horse. When a Micky D's comes into view, I take the exit.

I park, go inside and place my order. I'm soon armed with steaming hot coffee and two sausage McMuffins. I take my breakfast out to the patio to get some fresh air while I eat. The morning is cool and clear and I'm soaking up some sunshine when I feel something brush against my legs. *What the hell?* I look under the table and a pair of green eyes look back. I'm greeted with a subdued, "Meow."

"Why, you little dickens—where'd you come from?" I ask, as I pick up the yellow tabby and scratch its head. This one reminds me of a cat I had as a child. I remember the vet telling me that the color of the cat defines its personality. The yellow males are schmoozers; the females are more or less persnickety little creatures. This one must be a male; he's rubbing against me like there's no tomorrow purring like crazy and licking my fingers. When I offer him a piece of McMuffin, he gobbles it down in one bite and looks up into my face begging for more. Nothing persnickety about this feline, and I can't resist his charm—he gets the rest of that McMuffin.

"Here ya go, you little moocher," I say. "In fact,

that's a good name for you. I forthwith christen you Moochy!"

• • •

With my little wayfarer friend contently perched on the bench next to me munching away, I open the manila envelope and unfold and reread the note being careful to preserve prints if any there be. I'm still perplexed. What would Steve have to do with a Senate vote? My attention is diverted when a group of rambunctious teens drive into the parking lot and clamber from their cars. As I watch them head for the entrance laughing and good naturedly jostling each other, I notice the newspaper stand adjacent the entrance of the restaurant. The headlines read:

U.S. SENATE TO VOTE TUESDAY ON COAL PHASE-OUT BILL.

Tuesday? I go to the stand and purchase a newspaper. Taking it back to my table, I read the article.

The hotly contested coal phase-out bill continues to loom in the balance as the ninety-one day deadline draws near. When the bill was introduced three months ago authorizing the United States to become the thirty-first country to join the Powering Past Coal Alliance (PPCA), it appeared there were enough votes in the

House and the Senate in favor of its enactment. It now looks as though the favorable vote will not be a slam dunk. Sources close to Kentucky Senator Mitchell Ratcliff indicate he is planning to withdraw his vote in favor of the bill and vote against it.

Senator Ratcliff's withdrawal, according to one of his aids, is supported by his reluctance to phase-out coal power generation without having a viable substitute in place before doing so. Recently, the senator stated "Coal is still the cheapest and most abundant source of energy and can be mined and burned with little environmental impact. It provides over half of the electricity used in the nation each day. In Kentucky, the electrical rates are the second lowest in the nation because of coal."

Oh, my God! Now it all makes sense. Steve just invested a fortune in crude oil futures. I saw the contracts on his desk... I've got to get help...

After carefully reading the note once more, I slip it back into the manila envelope. When I withdraw my hand I scratch my knuckle on the prongs on the flap. "Ouch!" I yelp, and Moochy stops licking his paws long enough to look up at me. "It's okay," I say and rub the little guy's head to reassure him. When I fold the prongs back to ensure I won't be scratched again, I notice they have something unusual attached to them. I closely examine the small round metal object. Suddenly, I remember during orientation at the CIA, recruits are given several crash courses, one of which included identifying tracking devices. I instantly recognize the object attached to the envelope flap as a tracking device. *So that's how they've been keeping tabs on me.*

When panic grips me, whether it was paranoia, instinct, or just plain fear, I look across the parking lot in the direction of the entrance. The car I spot turning into the driveway looks like one of the plain, unmarked government vehicles used by the CIA. Even at this distance, I can see that this one has a white paint smear on the right front fender. I duck under the table to avoid detection.

Moochy, probably thinking I'm playing, joins me in my hiding place and rubs against me. Just then, I have an epiphany. I reach up and grab the envelope from the tabletop and peel the tracking device off of the flap and press it into the fur on the top of Moochy's head. He doesn't even flinch. The glue that held it in place on the envelope is almost nonexistent and the device is just hanging by a thread. Hopefully that one little thread will give me enough time to make my grand escape.

"Shoo," I say and try to push Moochy out from under the table. He must think I'm playing with him because he turns over on his back as if inviting me to scratch his tummy.

"No! You go on. Get outta here," I scold. He's reluctant to leave, so I give him a swat and hiss at him, "Shoo, get on outta here."

If cats can express hurt feelings, I think I just saw it. He eventually takes the hint and saunters out from under the table. He stops, looking back at me once, and then proceeds toward the trash dumpster. I watch the tracking device bobble around on top of his head with his every step. I can only hope the device stays put long enough to give me a head start.

"That's it, good boy. Just keep on going," I whisper, while making shooing motions with my hands.

My attention is now drawn back to the suspected CIA vehicle. It's slowly circling the restaurant, and as it passes, I recognize Watson and Samuels. They must have figured out I was on the hotel airport shuttle and connected the dots. At least they don't know what my rental looks like—yet.

Out of the corner of my eye I watch Moochy jump up onto the dumpster at the far end of the parking area. Watson immediately turns his car that direction. I can see Samuels' lips moving. He must be monitoring the tracking screen and directing Watson. Before they get very far, a garbage truck barrels into the driveway and makes a show of backing up to the dumpster. It's maneuvering between where I parked and the CIA car. Using the garbage truck as a cover, I make a dash for my rental. Before I clear the parking lot and enter the stream of traffic, I look back. Moochy, apparently frightened by the beeping and backing of the garbage truck, jumps out of the dumpster. I see him make a beeline in the opposite direction. *Good boy. Keep the CIA at bay for me.*

CHAPTER THREE

Tag, You're It...

"Where'd she go?" Watson asks.

"Can't tell. She's not moving… No, wait, there she goes." Samuels replies and points to the exit.

"All I see is the garbage truck." Watson says.

"Yeah, she must be in front of it. Well, at least the device is still working."

Watson careens his neck trying to look around the garbage truck. "You still have 'er on radar?" he asks.

"Yep. Soon as the truck clears the parking lot, we'll have her in our sights."

When the garbage truck stops at the exit of the parking lot and makes a left turn, Watson and Samuels sit in stunned silence; there's no vehicle in front of the truck.

"Where the hell did she go?" Watson asks swiveling his head left and then right.

Samuels, rubbing the stubble on his chin, snorts, "She duped us, Sherlock. Must've found the device and tossed it into the dumpster. No telling how far ahead of us she is by now."

"Great! You get to tell Cunningham while I buy us tickets to someplace where we'll never be found."

● ● ●

Once I clear the parking lot, I keep checking my rearview mirror to ensure I'm not being followed. So far, so good but I still don't know what I'm going to do. Dodging my nemesis has been a full time job, and now that I'm confident I'm not being followed, I can concentrate on devising a plan. I'm so absorbed in my thoughts that I don't realize I'm speeding. When I see the flashing lights approaching from behind, I check my speedometer—20 miles over the limit. *Oh, no! That's just what I don't need!* My nerves are shattered and I'm so unstrung that I start crying as I pull over and lower my window.

"Where's the fire?" the trooper asks, approaching the driver's side of my vehicle.

I'm too distraught to answer and just sit and sob.

The trooper, ignoring my distress, says, "Driver's license?"

I'm shaking so violently I'm unable to extract my license from the slot in my wallet. The trooper, apparently realizing I'm not putting on a show to get out of a ticket, asks, "Hey, little lady, are you okay?"

I shake my head. "No, I…I…I'm being followed…" I manage to stutter.

I glance up and see him look back at the oncoming traffic. A moment later he asks, "Who's following you?"

"Two CIA agents," I blurt, and from the look on his face I realize he probably thinks I'm some kind of kook.

"Un-huh. And why are they following you?"

"They want to kill me..."

I watch disbelief leap into his eyes. "Un-huh. And why would they want to do that?"

"It's a long story and I...I...I need help."

The trooper hooks his thumbs over his duty belt and looks around again as traffic whizzes by. Then, looking back at me, he says, "Ruby Tuesday's is up this way about a quarter of a mile. Follow me to the next exit and you can tell me your story over lunch." I'm conflicted and he apparently notices. "You can trust me. After all, our mission is to serve and protect—it says so on my rear bumper." The trooper turns back toward his cruiser. Before he's out of earshot, he shouts, "Don't try anything. My rig is faster than yours and it won't bode well for you if you attempt to flee."

I nod. *Where would I go anyway?*

• • •

I park next to the cruiser and the trooper escorts me to the door. We enter Ruby Tuesday's, and once we're seated, a waitress approaches. "Afternoon, Tag," she says to the trooper and then smiles at me. Pencil in hand, she looks back at the trooper, "The usual?"

"Afternoon, Cindy. Yep, I'll have the usual," and he hands his menu back to Cindy. They both look at me with questioning eyes. Since I just ate, I pass on lunch and order iced tea.

"Coming right up," Cindy says. She closes her order pad and slips it into her uniform pocket. Placing the pencil back behind her ear, she gathers the menus and retreats.

As I sit across the table from my rescuer, I examine him for the first time. He's the quintessential tall, dark and handsome icon that women swoon over. His nametag identifies him as Trooper Britt Taggert. He must have noticed me sizing him up because he points to his nametag. "My friends just call me Tag." After a pause, he asks, "And what's your name?"

Now that I've settled down and am able to function again, instead of answering, I remove my driver's license from my wallet and hand it to him.

Studying it carefully, Tag says, "Hum, Megan Lavon Duval, twenty-six years old, five feet five inches, one hundred thirty pounds, blond hair, blue eyes." He hands the license back and asks, "Now, why would the CIA want to harm you?"

Before I can answer, Cindy is back with our order. I'm surprised when she places a cobb salad before Tag. I would have guessed him to be a burger and fries kind of guy. He must have noticed my expression. Drizzling a light vinaigrette dressing over his salad, he says, "Actually, I'm not one of those health freaks. I eat light at lunch saving the carbs and calories so I can relax over a hefty dinner." After taking the first bite, he continues, "Now, you were saying…"

I pull the newspaper from my purse and show him the article on the upcoming coal phase-out congressional vote. "This," I say and point to the piece. "is what they're trying to promote. That way, coal will no longer be the competition and oil will reign supreme."

He pauses between bites and looks across the table at the article I'm displaying. "Okay. So where do you fit in?" he asks, and then continues to devour his salad.

Refolding the newspaper, I cram it back into my shoulder bag. Eager to confide in someone who can help, I blurt out the whole story in quick short sentences. "Jess picked some guy's pocket at the mall. She didn't know what she was getting into. By the time I got to her place she was already dead."

"Wait," Tag says, holding up a restraining hand. "Who's Jess?"

"Jess was my college roommate and best

friend." I take a deep breath and continue, "She must have mailed the envelope to me the afternoon before she was murdered."

Pausing with his fork poised in mid-air, Tag furrows his brow and asks, "Jess was murdered? How do you know that?"

"Because, when I went to her place I found her body…"

"Okay, this isn't working. I'm too confused. Back up and slow down—start from the beginning."

I nod. My mouth is suddenly dry so I take a gulp of tea. Starting over, I relate the whole story as the events took place. At the conclusion, I sweep my arm around encompassing the interior of the restaurant and say, "And now here we are."

Tag has long since finished his salad and leans forward on crossed arms apparently absorbing every word. He finally says, "Wow! That's a lot to lay on a guy who just wanted to issue you a speeding ticket."

I can't help it and laugh out loud. The lightheartedness was short-lived, and in my desperation, I look into Tag's eyes and ask, "Will you help me?"

"If I can," he says. "What's the plan?"

"That's the problem, I don't have one. I've been too busy trying to stay alive to even think about how to prevent the assassination."

"Have you tried calling the senator's office?"

"No. I haven't had the chance, and besides it's the weekend…"

"Right! Probably no one would be there." After a slight pause, Tag asks, "Is there anyone at the CIA you can trust?"

"No! Not after all that's happened. I trusted Steve. That's why I made a beeline for the CIA when I thought I was being stalked. Steve sure had me fooled. I thought he was a standup guy. Now I don't even trust my instincts and am suspicious of everyone."

Tag, with a thoughtful expression, looks around the restaurant. I've noticed him doing this several times since we met. That must be his way of buying time to think. He finally says, "My shift ends at four this afternoon and then I have a three-day break before my next shift. Today is Saturday and since Tuesday is the deadline, if we're going to foil the assassination, we'll have to get a move on."

I feel like jumping up and hugging him I'm so relieved to finally have someone I feel I can depend on in my corner. Before I can say another word, Tag stands, puts a few bills on the table, offers me his hand and we head for the door.

When we're outside, Tag says, "It isn't safe for you to be out in the open with murderous

CIA agents lurking about. I live pretty close so I suggest you hole up at my place until the end of my shift. Afterwards, we'll put our heads together and see if we can come up with a plan to prevent the assassination, and at the same time make sure you're safe."

• • •

I follow Tag to his apartment complex. His home is tastefully appointed and neat and tidy—not at all what I expect a bachelor pad to look like. "Very nice," I remark, as I set my purse on a small table in the entry way.

"Thank you. My mother is an interior decorator and gets all the credit. There's snacks in the pantry and drinks in the 'frig. Help yourself to whatever you like. I'll be back about four-thirty or five." He goes to the door and looks back at me before exiting, "You gonna be okay?"

"Yes. Thank you…I feel safe here."

He gives me a salute as he leaves. I hear him try the lock after closing the door behind him. Kicking off my shoes, I curl up on the sofa and turn on the TV. I'm suddenly on full alert when I hear the announcer introduce a segment on the upcoming coal phase-out bill in the Senate. "It appeared the bill would pass until Senator Ratcliff announced he would be voting against it." A sense of urgency swarms me and I don't hear the rest of what the announcer is saying. *We've just got to do something...and quickly.*

Feeling exhausted and helpless, extreme anxiety and dread engulfs me. Unable to cope with the situation any longer, I must have dozed off because the next thing I know Tag is gently shaking my shoulder.

"Wake up, Meg," he says. "I have a plan."

"What? Where...where am I?"

"It's me, Tag. You fell asleep..."

I rub my eyes trying to get my bearings. "Oh, yeah. Now I remember." And the memory regarding the upcoming coal phase-out vote I watched on TV this afternoon rushes to the forefront of my mind.

"Tag, we're running out of time," I blurt and hasten to tell him about the segment. After a pause, I say, "You said you have a plan?"

"Yes, I do, and I think it'll work."

CHAPTER FOUR

Hopscotch...

I'm now wide awake and back into the reality of our situation. "What's this plan of yours?" I ask, as I sit up.

Tag sits down beside me. "Do you know if the senator has bodyguards?"

I think a moment before answering. "It would be uncommon for a congressman to have security unless he or she had been threatened. The threat to Ratcliff's life has not been revealed so I wouldn't think so—that is, unless the senator hired someone on his own."

"Um-hum," Tag says, and gives me a serious look. "How brave are you?"

"What? Brave, what do you mean brave?" I stammer. "And why do I have to be brave?" I shudder, recalling the events of the last twenty-four hours.

Taking my hand, Tag says, "We can't involve anyone else. If the faction out there is working through the CIA, we can't afford to trust anyone. I hate to break the news to you but we'll have to do this on our own."

My lips quiver when I say, "Oh, my God! Do

what on our own?"

Tag holds my hand tighter. "Intercept the senator as he enters the chambers on Tuesday, that is if we are unable to alert him before then."

I jerk my hand from Tag's grip and jump up. Tag intently watches me as I pace the floor. I finally remark, "You realize they know who I am and what I look like. I'd be a sitting duck…"

Tag grabs my hand as I pass in in front of him and pulls me back down next to him. "Easy Meg. I've thought of that. Our first stop will be the mall."

The mall?

Apparently, noticing the perplexed expression on my face, he rushes on. "We'll buy you a wig and some other stuff to use as a disguise. In a disguise, you'll be free to move around and not have to worry about being recognized when we enter the Senate Chambers."

I just stare at him and the smug look he has on his face. He's probably feeling smart that he came up with this plan. "Sure, easy for you to say," I retort.

Tag rears back against the sofa cushions and props his feet up on the coffee table, "Cowboy up, Meg! We're duty bound to give it our best shot."

I've had enough close calls the past two days to last a lifetime. Now the thought of voluntarily jumping off the cliff makes me nauseous. "Hold on there, Die Hard, you may be duty bound but I didn't take an oath to serve and protect…"

In a more serious tone, Tag pleads, "I can't do it without your help, Meg. If the bad guys are still looking for you, where will you hide anyway? And even after the hit, if they succeed, they'll be out to get you because you know too much and have the evidence to nail their asses. Think about it and let me know." Then, looking at his watch, he says, "You have five seconds to decide."

• • •

It's after midnight when we hit D.C. and raining buckets.

"You know you can't go home," Tag says.

"I know."

"There's a Hyatt pretty close to the Capitol Building. We can get rooms there…"

I'm so tired I can barely keep my eyes open, "That's fine," I mumble.

"We have tomorrow and Monday to try to contact Senator Ratcliff."

• • •

Tag procures two rooms at the Hyatt and after he parks the car, escorts me to my room. It must be the cop in him because he comes in and takes a quick tour ensuring everything is secure before leaving for his room. I'm now so paranoid that I double check the door after he leaves to make sure it's locked.

In my mad rush to leave the Holiday, I didn't take time to grab my suitcase. Consequently, I have few personal items with me. The Hyatt provides guests with a small tube of toothpaste and tiny bottles of shampoo and hair conditioner. *Better than nothing.* I brush my teeth with my finger, shower, wash my hair and put my jeans and T-shirt back on. I'm so beat by this time, I don't even turn the sheets back; I just flop down and am soon fast asleep.

• • •

The hub-bub of the motel coming alive awakens me. Feeling much better after a good night's sleep, I open my eyes and stretch. I'm just coming alive and recognize Tag's voice when he knocks on my door and asks, "Are you awake?" I really didn't think he'd boogie out on me, but relief washes over me when I hear his voice and I rush to the door. Tag is standing in the hallway holding two Starbuck's cups. I grab the front of his shirt and pull him into the room.

"You're a lifesaver," I say.

"Well, good morning to you, too," he replies, and hands me one of the Starbuck cups.

It's then I realize I could've been more

appreciative and blush with embarrassment. "Thank you," I say. "You're a lifesaver in more ways than one."

"At your service, ma'am." He says and points to the small round table in front of the floor to ceiling window. Before he sits down, he pulls open the drapes. The morning looms wet from last night's rain and everything looks fresh and new glistening in the late autumn sun.

I suddenly long for the time when I didn't have a care in the world—and that was only two days ago. Tears well up in my eyes as I remember Jess, and I quickly brush those thoughts aside. I have to stay focused. "Where do we go from here?" I ask.

Tag sets his cup on the table and pulls a slip of paper from his shirt pocket and hands it to me. "I accessed one of the public computers in the lobby while I waited for our coffee and managed to retrieve Senator Ratcliff's home address. He lives in Herndon, Virginia. That's about forty minutes from here."

I study the slip of paper, "Phone number?"

"Not available, probably unlisted."

"Umm, that's too bad," I say and then add, "Good work. At least we now have something to go on."

"Okay then, drink up and let's get to it!"

"Right! The sooner we get this over with, the better I'll feel."

Tag slips the paper back into his shirt pocket and stands. "First stop is the mall to put together a disguise—just in case his place is being staked out."

"Ten-four, good buddy," I say.

Tag laughs, "That went out with Smoky and the Bandit…" Then, apparently noticing me flush with embarrassment, he adds, "Corny…but cute."

• • •

Because it's Sunday, the only store we find open this early is a Walmart. As soon as we pull into a parking slot, I say, "I've done a lot of shopping at Walmart and know my way around the store. If you want to wait here, I'll run in and pick up a few things."

"Works for me," Tag says. "I hate to shop."

Inside the store I grab a shopping cart and head directly for the women's department. I quickly scan the racks of garments and select a navy blue skirt with a matching jacket, and add a white blouse. I then go to the shoe department and find a pair of medium heel black pumps.

On the way in, I noticed Halloween items in the clearance aisle. After selecting a suitable ensemble in the clothing department, I head that direction hoping to find something to use as a disguise.

Rummaging through the assortment of costumes, I can't believe my luck when I find a package with a picture of a rock star on the front. She's made up with long black hair, exaggerated black eye lashes, and posing in a pair of black fishnet hosiery, topped off with a sexy black lace teddy. The package contains the identical items as pictured on the front. I add the package to my collection and then make a pass through the cosmetic aisle.

In less than 30 minutes I'm out of the store.

"That didn't take long," Tag says, with surprise in his voice. "You find everything okay?"

"Indeed I did."

• • •

It's starting to rain again as we leave the Walmart parking lot headed for the senator's home in Herndon. Since it's Sunday, traffic is pretty light this time of day. Before we reach the senator's residence, putting modesty aside, I wriggle out of my jeans and T-shirt and pull on the Walmart skirt and blouse. Using the visor mirror, I apply a generous amount of makeup, the eyelashes and the wig. I use the picture of the rock star on the package as a guide.

When I finish, I ask Tag, "How do I look?"

He takes his eyes off of the highway for a moment and glances at me. He then immediately takes another look, "Who are you, strange lady?"

I flip the long, black hair of the wig back over my shoulder in true rock star fashion and smirk, "You must be a geek from another planet. I thought everyone knew me."

We share a much needed laugh.

"All kidding aside, you look amazing. Don't think I would have recognized you if I didn't know better."

"That's reassuring. I feel safer now." Taking another look in the visor mirror, I apply another coat of lipstick and say, "This is actually fun. I could get used to being a celeb."

"Ten minutes into the role and already fame and fortune are going to your head."

"Eat your heart out—remember, this was your idea!"

• • •

It's still raining when we reach Herndon. Using the GPS in Tag's SUV we locate the senator's residence. It's a red brick mansion in the upscale part of town. Tag drives slowly up the street surveilling the premises. At the end of the cul-de-sac he turns and makes another pass by the senator's residence.

"Looks pretty normal," he says. "If it's being watched, it's not obvious."

"Well, they could be in the house across the

street…"

"Maybe, but we don't have time to analyze every possibility. We're rapidly running out of time."

Tag pulls into the driveway and kills the engine.

"You wait here, I'm going to see if the senator is available."

"NO!" Terror grips me as I look around behind us. The fear I experienced the last two days I spent running for my life resurfaces. "I mean, I don't want to be left alone."

Pointing to the portico, Tag says, "I'll be just a few yards away. Besides, I brought roscoe, just in case," and he pats the gun tucked into his waistband. "You're safe, at least for the time being. Don't think you'll be recognized and they certainly won't recognize the car since it's mine."

Tag pats my hand, turns up his jacket collar against the rain and eases out of the car. I crunch down lower into the seat and watch his every move. He rings the bell, and as he waits, he glances back toward the car and smiles at me. I'm reassured by his positive attitude. A few moments later a middle-aged woman dressed in a modest maid's uniform opens the door. I can't hear the conversation mainly because of the rain pounding on the roof of the car. After a brief exchange the maid shakes her head and closes the door. Tag takes the steps two at a time and runs through the rain back to the car.

"What happened?" I ask in an anxious voice as soon as he closes the car door.

Wiping rain from his face with his handkerchief, he replies, "The Ratcliffs went to the Bahamas for a few days. They won't be back until late tomorrow."

"Oh, no! Is there any way we can contact the senator in the Bahamas?"

"The maid wouldn't give out that information even if she had it."

"Did you tell her it was a matter of life and death?"

"Yes. She just smirked and mumbled something like 'They all say that,' then she closed the door in my face."

Tag starts the car and we head back the way we came. When he stops at an intersection waiting to pull into the stream of traffic, I thought I saw the same government car that had been pursuing me turn onto the street. It was raining so hard my view was distorted as rain sluiced down the windows. I couldn't even see if the suspect car had the trace of white paint on the fender. As it passed Tag's SUV, I turned my head and watched out the back window. Even through the torrent of rain, I could see the vehicle turn into the senator's driveway.

"Tag, I think that was Watson and Samuels in the car that just passed us."

In the time it took me to alert Tag, he had already merged onto the interstate and there's no way to turn around at this juncture. I realize we'll have to go to the next exit in order to retrace our steps.

"Are you sure?" he exclaims, maneuvering the vehicle into the flow of traffic.

"Pretty sure. Even though their features were distorted by the rain, they looked like a couple of faces I don't think I'll ever forget."

"Dammit! When they find out the senator isn't home, they'll most likely be gone by the time we get turned around and make it back." Then after a pause, "Hope they didn't see us leaving the senator's residence. I'd rather they not get a fix on our transportation."

It took about forty-five minutes to get to the next exit and backtrack, mainly because we were stopped while cars and debris were being cleared from an accident scene. When we finally drive past the senator's home, everything appears to be quiet and there are no cars in the driveway.

"Guess they got the same brushoff I did," Tag says, as he rounds the cul-de-sac and we turn back toward D.C.

CHAPTER FIVE

Cops & Robbers...

"You hungry?" Tag asks as we approach the city.

"As a matter of fact," I exclaim, "I am. You must've heard my tummy growl."

Tag takes the next exit. In the distance I see the famous restaurant, *Founding Fathers*. I'd heard raves about their seafood but had never been there.

"You like seafood?" Tag asks, glancing at me.

"You bettcha."

"Well then, game on," Tag says as he pulls into the parking lot.

• • •

The interior of the *Founding Fathers* is tastefully decorated with framed replicas of the Declaration of Independence, the Articles of Confederation, the U.S. Constitution, and many other historical documents. Interspersed on the walls between the documents are portraits of the original founding fathers: Alexander Hamilton, John Adams, Benjamin Franklin, John Jay, Thomas Jefferson, James Madison and George Washington.

"Very impressive," I say. The maître d' seats us and then disappears back to his station at the front entrance.

Soon a waiter appears and hands us menus. "Can I start you off with something to drink?" he asks.

Tag raises his brow looking in my direction. I shake my head. "Just water for now," he says and the waiter retreats.

Since it's between lunch and dinner, we virtually have the place to ourselves. I watch Tag look around sizing up the venue. Turning back to me, he says, "This is one of my favorite places. It reminds me of the men who were brave enough to live and die for what they believed." Tag then takes my hand across the table, "I hope you realize, Meg, that may well be what we're doing."

I nod. "Since Jess' murder and having to run for my life the past few days, that thought has been niggling me as well—to say the least. Your words give me a whole new perspective." My silver service rattles when I pound the table with a clenched fist, declaring, "If it comes to that, I'll join the founding fathers…"

Tag laughs at my melodrama. "Hopefully, it won't come to that."

Tag's courage makes me braver and upon mustering my resolve, I know I can do whatever it takes to prevent the assassination. Tag again squeezes my hand, and I'm now seeing him through different eyes. I search his face and look deep into his eyes. He's not just a state trooper who came to my rescue, he's a true-blue dedicated patriot—a man of principle and honor and backs up his words with action. *I think I'm falling in love.*

• • •

After lunching on seafood combination plates, we waddle out to the car. I'm so stuffed I can barely breathe—my Walmart skirt feels like it shrank a size.

"Where to now?" I query, groaning as I fasten my seatbelt.

"We have no choice but to wait. I guess we could make another run past the senator's home late tomorrow evening to see if he's back yet. Otherwise, we'll have to try to intercept him when he arrives at the Capitol Building on Tuesday." After a brief pause, Tag asks, "Do you know what the senator looks like?"

"Not really. I've never seen him in person. We could probably access a photo of him on the Internet."

Tag nods. "Since my place is fairly close to the Capitol Building we can spend the night there and get an early start. We'll pull him up on my computer and see what he looks like."

● ● ●

By the time we finish our research, it's almost 9:00 p.m. We were able to access a bio on Senator Mitchell Ratcliff which included a photograph. His outstanding feature is his head of unruly red hair. After studying the photograph, Tag remarks, "Well, at least, he'll be easy to spot in a crowd."

"That he will," I say and yawn.

"Guess that's all we can do for now," Tag says, and shuts down the computer. "We should call it a night. Who knows what tomorrow will bring and we need to be rested and ready for whatever awaits us."

The last few days have been laced with bad experiences and when Tag says *ready for whatever awaits us* I shudder. I think I know all too well what in all likelihood awaits us. Forcing negative thoughts from my mind, I stand and smooth the wrinkles from my skirt. Not sure where my quarters are, I look around. Tag takes my hand and leads me to the bedroom. "You take the bedroom. I'll crash on the sofa."

"But…that doesn't seem fair," I reply.

"Where'd you get the idea life is fair? And don't argue with me," Tag says, and points to the bathroom. "Take a shower if you like…" and with that, he steps out into the hallway and closes the door behind him.

I stare after him for a moment. I then place my Walmart bag of meager belongings on the bed and head for the bathroom. After I shower, I wrap in a towel and dump the contents of the sack out onto the bed looking for something to sleep in. I zero in on the black lace teddy and fishnet stockings and have an immediate change of plan. *Why not!*

A few minutes later, dressed in my rock star garb, I sashay into the living room. Tag has kicked back with his feet on the coffee table watching the news when I enter. When he looks up, his chin drops and his eyes grow wide, "What the hell," he says. Then smiling, he adds, "If you're trying to seduce me, you're doing a pretty damn good job."

• • •

When I awake the next morning, Tag is already up and the aroma of fresh brewed coffee is wafting through the apartment. He appears in the bedroom doorway holding two mugs with a newspaper tucked under his arm.

Although I don't remember doing so, sometime during the night I must have traded my black lace teddy for one of Tag's soft, white T-shirts.

"Déjà vu," I say, and prop myself up on the pillows. "Didn't we just do this?" I remark, referring to him having brought the Starbuck's to my motel

room the previous day.

"Hum, close but not quite the same," Tag replies, and shoots me a sly smile. I feel myself flush. Tag sets his mug on the nightstand and hands me the other one. He then fluffs his pillow and props himself up beside me on the bed making a show of shaking the newspaper open. Within seconds, he bolts up causing coffee to slosh from my mug.

"Oh, my God!" he exclaims.

"What! What is it?" I ask, sopping up spilled coffee with some tissues I grab from a box on the nightstand. Tag turns the paper for me to see. The headlines read:

SENATOR MITCHELL RATCLIFF'S MAID FOUND MURDERED.

Watson and Samuels? "Oh, no!" I exclaim, and stretch my neck to better see the paper. Tag reads the article out loud.

The body of Marcella Hernandez, longtime maid of U.S. Senator Mitchell Ratcliff, was discovered late yesterday evening at the Ratcliff's Herndon, Virginia, home. The Ratcliffs, upon their return from a short vacation in the Bahamas, found the dead body of their maid fully clothed in the bathtub. She had apparently drowned.

Preliminary reports indicate the victim may have been subjected to water board torture before she died. Her arms and hands were bruised and scratched indicating she put up a struggle. The authorities are treating Hernandez' death as a homicide. No suspects have yet been identified and the Ratcliffs state they have no idea who would want to harm Hernandez.

The victim immigrated to the United States from Honduras ten years ago and had been employed by the Ratcliffs that entire time. Hernandez was sixty-two years old and has no known living relatives.

Senator Ratcliff has been criticized for reversing his decision to vote in favor of a bill authorizing the United States to join with thirty other countries in establishing a coalition known as the Powering Past Coal Alliance. The proposed phase-out bill comes before the Senate tomorrow for a vote. His reason for reversal, as previously reported, is his reluctance to phase-out the use of coal as a means of power generation because, as he has stated, it is the cheapest and most abundant source of energy and no viable alternative *energy source has yet been developed. "Under the circumstances," the senator announced, "I cannot in good conscience lend my name to such a bill."*

Because of the circumstances surrounding the homicide of the senator's maid, the FBI has been called in to assist in the investigation.

I'm stunned. The last few days have taken their toll on my psyche, and feeling guilty that we may have been the cause of the maid's death, I begin to cry. "We probably led them to her!"

Tag takes me in his arms. "Very unlikely. They couldn't have followed us because there is no way they could have known what my car looked like. The hit was already out on the senator and they probably tracked him down the same way we did."

Tag gently strokes my hair comforting me. He finally says, "I suspect her murder has something to do with the proposed coal phase-out bill. Although the paper doesn't say so, the killers obviously weren't there to burglarize the premises. When she informed me she was unable to contact the senator, I had no reason to disbelieve her. Apparently, the killers were not of the same mind and tried to force the information from her." Tag looks at the clock. "Come on, Meg. Get dressed. We're running out of time."

Coming face-to-face with two murders, Jess' and the senator's maid, causes me to rethink my previous resolve. When reality sets in, I wonder if I'm ready to die for my country. *Do I really want to do that?* "Maybe we could…" I stop midsentence when I see the look on Tag's face and do a complete turnaround. "Maybe… we should make every effort to stop the assassination," I blurt, and jump out of bed headed for the bathroom.

● ● ●

I'm decked out in my now familiar disguise when we arrive at our destination. Tag drives through the parking lot on the off-chance the CIA vehicle may already be here and I may possibly recognize it. I don't see it.

When we exit Tag's car, he takes my hand and we walk toward the entrance of the Capitol Building. Not sure if the gesture is to reassure me or to keep me from backing out. Watching government employees rush past apparently scurrying to get to work on time, I'm nervous and feeling exposed even in my disguise. When several people stop and stare at me, I wonder if it's because I look like a freak or because I look like that iconic rock star.

"How are we going to do this?" I ask. "I'm

assuming Ratcliff will be surrounded by bodyguards after the murder of his maid."

"My thoughts exactly. And we won't be able to get within twenty feet of him."

"The upside is the assassins won't either," I muse.

"Their best bet would be to try to gun him down from the chamber balcony. His red hair is a distinguishing feature they can zero in on. It's like having a target painted on him. If they're smart, they'll make the hit and execute a getaway when the chamber is reduced to utter chaos."

"Is that what you'd do?"

Tag scans the exterior of the building for a few moments. "Yes. There're so many entrances, it's unlikely they'd know which one the senator would use. They'd have to have pretty good backup to cover all the doors. And as far as we know, there are only two of them. However, it's for certain when he's in the chamber he'll be a sitting duck."

I cringe. Now that the moment is upon us, my resolve is waning.

Tag, apparently sensing my reluctance, turns me toward him and looks me in the eye, "You still with me, Tiger?" It was more of a statement than a question.

I'm suddenly filled with shame for even

thinking of quitting on him. After all he's done to help me and the senator, I can't let him down now. I remember when I was a kid I'd cross my fingers behind my back to ward off evil when I wasn't sure I could keep a promise, or occasionally, just for luck. Taking a deep breath, I cross my fingers when I say, "Damn bettcha!"

"That's my girl," Tag says and takes my arm ushering me into the building.

• • •

I recognize the interior of the Capitol Building once we're inside. Slipping my arm through Tag's, I say, "When I was in high school our senior trip was to D.C. We toured most of the government buildings including the Senate."

Feeling somewhat like a tour guide, I continue, "The Senate is in one wing of the Capitol Building and the House in the other. Since I've been here before I kinda know my way around. In the Senate wing there are stairs on both sides leading to the balcony and also an elevator." I pause a moment before adding, "I even know where the restrooms are."

"Well, look at you! You're just a wealth of information. Show me to the balcony," Tag prompts, with a broad smile. His humor helps ease the terror I've been experiencing ever since we arrived here.

The balcony completely surrounds the Senate floor and my heart swells with pride when I look down into the chamber. I'm proud to be an American and marvel at the insight and foresight the founders of our nation had when they wrote the Declaration of Independence , the U.S. Constitution, and the Bill of Rights. Visualizing beyond their years, they were able to define and incorporate language into the documents to help avoid potential disasters—even well into the future. Now, over two hundred years later, the words they penned still ring true. The wars fought over the years to preserve freedom, both at home and abroad, have cost too many lives for us to have let those brave Americans die in vain. God help us, we just can't let the bad guys win!

"Where should we sit?" I ask.

"Good question. I didn't realize the balcony was so large. It's hard to say where the assassins will locate." Tag gives me a stern look. "They may even split up so that they can have shots at him from different angles."

It doesn't take me long to connect the dots. "Oh, no. Don't tell me you think we should split up," I stammer.

"Calm down, Meg," Tag says in a reassuring voice. "I don't want us to split up but we can cover twice as much territory if we do. You know what

Watson and Samuels look like so you could signal me if you see them. I'll keep an eye on you from over there," Tag says and points to an area directly across from where I'm standing. "If I see anything suspicious from my side, I'm close enough to head it off."

His words do little to quell my concerns. My knees feel weak and my stomach churns. "But Watson and Samuels know what I look like…"

"Not now," Tag says. "You look so much like that rock star, you'll probably be swarmed by adoring fans seeking autographs."

I slip my hands into my jacket pockets and manage a stingy smile. Once again I'm drenched with guilt remembering how Tag saved me. *How can I let him down now?* Imitating that rock star, I flip my fake hair back over my shoulder with the back of my hand and ask, "Can I get in trouble for impersonating her?"

Tag laughs at my frivolity. "Hell, no. The costume company had to have her consent to manufacture her image. You're just a kook that idolizes her."

Now I manage a sincere smile. I even laugh. "Okay, I'll do it," I say.

• • •

As soon as Tag leaves my side, I regret having

agreed. I want to reach out and drag him back instead of watching him depart. I climb the stairs in the direction of the rear seats and take up a position where I can see most of the balcony. I scrunch as low in the seat as I can and yet still see the surrounding area. It doesn't take long for the balcony to fill. I guess all the publicity on the proposed coal phase-out bill has attracted more spectators than usual. I carefully scrutinize everyone who comes in. I don't see Watson or Samuels.

The balcony is now filled to capacity. I look down onto the chamber floor and see Senator Ratcliff kibitzing with some of his fellow senators. It occurs to me that he could be an easy target. Frustrated, I look across the balcony to where Tag is seated. *Oh, my God!* There right behind Tag I see Watson—and he's reaching inside his jacket for what could be a gun. My heart skips a few beats and then takes off like a rocket. I jump to my feet, and suddenly remembering a Clint Eastwood movie where, when the secret agents spot a weapon, they shout, "GUN, GUN." Now, finding myself in the midst of certain disaster, my mind flips into automatic and I screech at the top of my voice, "GUN, GUN!"

Tag must have seen the same movie. Much to my relief, he instantly leaps to his feet, and turns. Watson must have been spooked by my shouting and has already disappeared into the mass of screaming onlookers. From my perch, I watch two security guards tackle Tag and cuff him. *Oh, my God. They think Tag's the assassin!*

In a panic, I fight my way through the frenzied crowd as they climb over seats, pushing and shoving each other and blocking the aisles in an attempt to get out of the balcony. Finally, I make my way to the exit and run down the stairs hoping to stymie Tag's arrest. Unfortunately, I'm too late. There's no sign either of him or security on the main floor. The guards must have whisked him out a back entrance.

I evaluate my position and realize all I can do now is to find out where Tag's being taken and explain the situation to the authorities. Outside, I pause on the steps of the Capitol Building trying to put together a plan of action. I'm running low on cash—well that is cash of my own. I still have the ten thousand dollars hit money stashed in my purse. If need be, I'll use it to post bond for Tag.

Having left my rental in the parking lot of Tag's apartment building when we went to Herndon, I don't have transportation and my only choice is to attempt to retrieve my rental car. Rapidly descending the Capitol steps, I rush to the curb and hail a taxi. Even though I don't know Tag's address, I think I can guide the driver to Tag's apartment where I can pick up my rental.

A taxi screeches to a halt adjacent to where I'm standing and I jerk the passenger door open. Before I get the door closed, the driver asks, "Where to," as he engages the meter and begins to drive away.

"Don't know the address but I can direct you."

"Okay, lady," he says, "It's your dime."

CHAPTER SIX

Dodgeball...

Confused about my next step, I head for a motel as soon as I pick up the rental car. I need solitude and time to think of a plan to rescue Tag. Common sense tells me he's being held at the central detention facility in D.C. Having been employed at the CIA for the last five years, I've learned the skill of how to locate people. I now put my experience to work. I reason that, even if they let him make that obligatory one phone call, he wouldn't know where to reach me—so I'll find him. I owe him—not that it matters.

I search the yellow pages and jot down phone numbers I think I'll need before beginning to make calls. A few minutes into my search, I reach someone who knows where Tag is being held. The desk clerk at the police department informs me that the would-be assassin is incarcerated in the central detention facility in D.C. His arraignment is scheduled for nine o'clock tomorrow morning in front of Judge Virgil Cromwell.

I thank the clerk and look at my watch. It's too late now to rescue Tag so I turn on the television to see how the media is spinning the uproar in the

Senate Chambers. I flip through the channels and the incident is breaking news on every channel. Apparently all the news outlets were present in the chambers this afternoon because of the publicity surrounding the vote on the anticipated coal phase-out bill and the murder of Senator Ratcliff's maid.

As I watch one of the local channels, I'm suddenly startled when I hear my voice shouting 'GUN, GUN' from somewhere in the background. I sink lower into the chair remembering vividly how the balcony exploded into mayhem. Some of the footage looks like the filming of an earthquake because of the cameramen being jostled by the frightened spectators as they rush from the chamber. Watching the drama unfold, I cringe when I see how roughly security treated Tag. He was wrestled down and handcuffed before being led from the balcony.

I turn off the TV and flop down on the bed. The last couple of days have been too much; Jess' murder, Steve's betrayal, running for my life, Marcella Hernandez' murder, and now Tag's arrest. It's much too much to absorb, and curling up, I cry myself to sleep.

• • •

I rise early, and even though my sleep was haunted with dreadful nightmares, I feel somewhat refreshed. I hang my skirt and jacket in the bathroom hoping steam from the shower will eliminate some of the wrinkles. Much to my surprise, it works. After I shower and dress, I examine myself in the bathroom mirror. I cringe at the haggard reflection that stares back at me. My inexpensive Walmart outfit seems to be holding up better than I am. I must have lost a few pounds over the last couple of days as the skirt keeps slipping down around my hips. Looking for a quick solution, I rummage through my purse and find a safety pin which I use to take up the slack in the waist. I figure the jacket will cover the safety pin. However, I have no cure for the dark circles under my eyes and my pale, lifeless skin. Even my hair has lost its luster. I fear I may never recuperate and promise myself that if I survive this ordeal I'm going to spend a month at a spa.

Taking one last look around, I determine I'm as ready as I'm ever going to be. Shouldering my purse, I leave the room and head for the lobby to check out. After I check out and make my way to the exit, I notice the motel has a free continental breakfast. My stomach growls at the sight of food so I pause long enough to wrap a couple of sweet rolls in a paper napkin and get a cup of coffee to go.

• • •

Securing the coffee in the cup holder between the front seats, I eat the sweet rolls as I maneuver through traffic. When I down the last morsel, I feel rejuvenated. I arrive at the courthouse a little before nine and park in the adjacent parking garage. Before exiting my vehicle, I take one last look in the visor mirror. I'm still ghastly pale so I smear a dab of lipstick on each cheek before applying a fresh coat to my lips. I open the car door and vigorously brush crumbs from my skirt before slipping into my jacket.

Before I step out of my vehicle, I take a long look around at my surroundings. I rationalize it's highly unlikely Watson and Samuels will show up here, but who knows. I'm now feeling more exposed than ever and constantly look back over my shoulder as I make my way through the garage to the elevator.

I'm relieved when I arrive at Judge Cromwell's courtroom without incident. I take a seat in the front row and try to reign in my emotions. I'm fidgety and actually jump when the rear entrance door swings open. I look back and watch as a deputy ushers Tag into the courtroom. When Tag sees me, he ever so slightly nods his head in my direction. I take that gesture as a good omen and am instantly encouraged.

• • •

As soon as the bailiff calls the court to order, a person I assume to be the U.S. attorney, rises and requests permission to speak.

"Granted, Mr. McLean," Judge Cromwell says, pushing his glasses up on the bridge of his nose. "Please proceed!"

"Your Honor," U.S. Attorney McLean begins, "the People move to dismiss the charges against the defendant? Mr. Taggert."

"And on what grounds?" the judge asks, not even looking up from the file he has open on his desk.

McLean turns and looks in Tag's direction then back at the judge. "Your Honor, since Mr. Tagget's arrest, we've had an opportunity to view the video tapes collected from the Senate balcony security cameras." Shuffling through some of the papers he had previously placed on the podium before him, he continues. "When we interviewed the Capitol security guards, they stated that, at the time of the incident and during the ensuing chaos, it appeared to them that Mr. Taggert was the cause of the disruption. Mr. Taggert was taken into custody and charged with obstructing government operations, disorderly conduct, and resisting arrest.

"However, overnight we conducted an in-depth inspection of the video tapes which were recorded from different angles in the Senate Chamber and balcony at the time of the incident. Upon reviewing the tapes from all angles, we concluded Mr. Taggert did not incite the disturbance. Rather, it was initiated by an unknown female shouting 'Gun! Gun!' Mr. Taggert, a law enforcement officer, only reacted to what he surmised to be a threat."

Judge Cromwell slowly removes his glasses and places them on the desk in front of him. "Did the defendant say why he was at the scene at that particular time?" he asks.

"Yes. When asked, he said he was an off-duty state trooper and because of the recent publicity on the then pending coal phase-out bill, he was interested in the outcome."

"I see," the judge says as he repositions the file. "Is there a possibility of a refiling or are you asking the court to dismiss the charges with prejudice?"

The U.S. attorney looks back at Tag. "Your Honor, in light of the recent revelations, the people request the charges against the defendant, Britt Taggert, be dismissed with prejudice."

"Motion granted," Judge Cromwell says, and bangs his gavel. To Tag he says, "Your case is dismissed, Mr. Taggert. The charges can never be refiled. You're free to leave."

I breathe a sigh of relief and head toward the back of the courtroom. I want to meet Tag as soon as he's released from custody. However, before I clear the courtroom I hear the judge say, "One more thing, Mr. McLean, did the video reveal who caused the disruption?"

Since it was me, I freeze midstride, waiting for the answer.

"No, Your Honor," McLean responds. "The tape revealed that when an unknown female, who apparently was seated in the balcony, screamed 'Gun, gun,' everyone jumped up and began to scramble for the exits. The venue erupted into a jumble of bodies pushing and shoving each other and we were unable to sort out who was who and who said what at that point."

"I see," Judge Cromwell says. Adjusting his glasses back on his nose, he orders the bailiff to call the next case.

• • •

After Tag is released and we're back out on the street, I look at him, "Where do we go from here?"

Tag rubs the back of his neck with a thoughtful expression on his face. "That's a good question."

There's a newsstand on the corner, and as we approach, Tag points to the headlines in one of the newspapers. "Looks like Ratcliff tanked the coal phase-out bill with his dissenting vote." Tag purchases a copy of the paper, flips it open and reads the article aloud.

IN THE MIDST OF CHAOS...

The much publicized coal phase-out bill was voted upon in the Senate today and it appeared Senator Mitchell Ratcliff may have been the target of an attempted assassination before the vote was taken. Senator Ratcliff had been criticized for stating he would be flipping his vote, changing a yea to a nay, thus defeating the passage of the highly controversial coal phase-out bill.

When interviewed, some of the eyewitnesses who were present today in the Senate balcony stated they thought they saw a man pull a gun and aim it in the Senator's direction immediately before an unidentified woman stood and shouted "Gun! Gun!"

The Senate chamber erupted in chaos and spectators ran screaming from the balcony section of the chamber as two security guards subdued the individual who they thought was the would-be assassin. The individual was immediately arrested and taken into custody.

When order was restored, President of the Senate, Vice-President Reid Caldwell, called for a vote on the pending coal phase-out bill which was defeated by one vote—Senator Ratcliff's swing vote. When later interviewed, Senator Ratcliff stated that he refused to be bullied by those who use threats and intimidation to assert their will in order to influence the voting." The senator also stated that the murder of his longtime maid was under investigation and that the murder was no doubt related to the coal phase-out bill

"Your quick action saved the senator's life," Tag says, as he refolds the newspaper and places it back on the stand.

"Not me! You're the hero. You scared Watson off."

"That's my job," he smiles, "and I couldn't have done it without you. I hope you know that! Come on, we're still not safe." Tag must have noticed the confused look on my face. He quickly adds, "Even though the voting has concluded, we're still in possession of some incriminating evidence— evidence that could fry Watson, Samuels, and Cunningham or at least send them to prison for the rest of their lives."

"Oh!" I exclaim and immediately look around half expecting to see our nemesis barreling down on us. "Shouldn't we now turn the money and note over to law enforcement and let them do the investigation?"

"Absolutely. However, in the meantime, our lives are still at risk. We're what you call key witnesses. You know what that means? In fact, since they've eliminated Jess, we're the only *living* witnesses and we have the evidence to implicate Watson, Samuels, and Cunningham."

I gulp. The reality of the situation finally hits me. I've had firsthand experience and know what that crew is capable of. I grab Tag's hand, and pulling him behind me, I quicken my pace encouraging him to walk faster. "Let's get outta here and pronto!"

A few minutes later, we reach the car and once inside I feel more secure than out in the open on the streets and an easy target. Tag buckles up, and as he engages the ignition, he says, "I'm acquainted with the police chief. I've attended various law enforcement seminars with him. He seems to be a dedicated law enforcement officer and I feel we can trust him."

I nod. "Okay—if you think so."

"The cop-shop will be our first stop." Then looking at me, with genuine concern in his voice, he asks, "You okay?"

I nod again. "I'll certainly be glad to dump this hot potato onto someone else's lap."

• • •

At police headquarters when we're shown to Police Chief Nate Buchannan's office, he greets us and appears to be warm and friendly. We spend the next hour explaining the situation. Tag takes the lead and fills the Chief in on what has taken place up to this point. Chief Buchannan listens intently and only interrupts when he needs clarification. When I hand him the manila envelope, the Chief looks inside and raises his brows. He then carefully extracts the note with the tips of his thumb and forefinger as we sit and watch.

The Chief carefully replaces the note back into the envelope after reading it and asks, "Did either of you touch this?"

"No," I say. "In accordance with my CIA training, I used my tweezers to withdraw it from the envelope when I first discovered it." I look over at Tag and add, "It's been in my possession since I received it and he hasn't touched it either."

Buchannan nods. "I'll have it checked for prints along with the bills in the package." Then looking at me, he adds, "Ms. Duval, you said you knew the men you suspected to be the would-be assassins? Is that correct?"

I scoot forward in my chair eager for the opportunity to help in any way I can. "Yes. I recognized the one in the Senate balcony as Agent Eric Watson. However, I didn't see his partner, Agent Kenneth Samuels, at that time." After a slight pause, I add, "They're both CIA agents under the supervision of Deputy Director Steve Cunningham. I'm Steve's personal assistant and I've seen the two of them come to his office many times." I take a deep breath and exclaim, "I also recognized them as the ones who've been tailing me."

Looking more serious, Buchannan says, "Well, from what you've told me, especially the conversation you overheard in Cunningham's office, it's obvious Cunningham is in this up to his eyeballs. I'll put a rush on the fingerprint check— since all three are CIA agents, their fingerprints should be on file—we just need to verify they match the evidence." After a slight pause, he adds, "The two of you aren't safe on the streets. We have a safe-house we use for witnesses we feel may be in jeopardy. I suggest you both stay at the safe house until we get the rogue agents out of circulation. If the fingerprints match Cunningham, Watson and Samuels' prints, hopefully we'll have them locked up by tomorrow."

I sit stoic. Tomorrow seems like a long time to wait, especially since I'm the target. I look over at Tag, his expression is noncommittal. My musings are interrupted and I'm drawn back to the present when Buchannan buzzes his secretary and says, "Patti, send in Crawford and Harris." After he hangs up, he explains, "Crawford and Harris are two of our detectives who will escort you to the safe house and stand guard tonight. I'm sorry but you won't have time to pick up any of your personal items. Your residences are most likely being watched. Right now you're truly sitting ducks and these men are probably desperate since their identities are known and will stop at nothing to silence you. You won't be safe until we get them behind bars."

I'm suddenly weak and as cold as ice. Spots dance before my eyes. *Oh, no! I'm going to faint!*

"Chief," Tag says, "I've known you a long time and trust your integrity. However, under the circumstances, how do you know we can trust Crawford and Harris not to have been bought off?"

Suddenly, my instincts are on full alert and I notice a startled look cross Buchannan's face when Tag asks that question. It lasted just an instant, but long enough for me to become suspicious.

"Sadly enough, we don't," Buchannan replies. "However, they've been with the department a long time and both have exemplary records. Their backgrounds are solid." He pauses before adding with a mirthless smile, "That's about all we have to hang our hats on—too bad we don't have a crystal ball."

I'm concerned about the chief's attitude. Don't know if it's the wild ride we've been on over the last few days or just plain paranoia but something just doesn't feel right. Before I can express my concerns, there's a knock on the door and two men dressed in civilian attire enter.

"Ah, Detectives Crawford and Harris," the chief points to the men respectively, "meet Megan Duval and Britt Taggert." We shake hands all around.

Their handshakes are warm and their smiles are friendly, but I've been duped before and my guard is still up—I don't feel I can trust them. The look on Buchannan's face when Tag asked about their trustworthiness haunts me.

Buchannan addresses the detectives. "We're providing protection for these two witnesses. I want you to take them to the safe house…"

With a puzzled look on his face, Crawford asks, "What safe house?"

Buchannan flushes at that remark and sirens start screaming in my head. *What the hell is going on. I gotta get outta here.* I look behind me at the closed door, but when I start to rise, Tag puts a restraining hand on my arm.

"The one on Canal Street!" Buchannan barks.

"Ah, oh, of course," Harris says, and I watch him give Crawford a look that says shut up and go with it.

A moment later, Buchannan is back in control. In a much more subdued voice, he says to the detectives, "Not sure how long it will take to make arrests. I'll have you relieved tomorrow morning."

"Roger that," Harris remarks and walks to the door and opens it.

We take the hint and when we rise to leave, Chief Buchannan rounds his desk and accompanies us out into the corridor. "We'll immediately get an APB out for the three musketeers. We have the element of surprise on our side so it shouldn't take long to round 'em up."

"Thank you, Chief," Tag says, and the two men shake hands.

The two detectives are a few paces ahead of us when we exit the police station. "Tag," I whisper, but before I can say anymore, he tightly squeezes my arm and I shut up. I try to pull away but Tag has a tight grip on me. He looks at me and barely shakes his head indicating for me to play along. I'm now sure he's picked up on the odd exchange between Buchannan and the detectives so I place my trust in him and let him lead me—hopefully not to the slaughter.

• • •

As soon as everyone has cleared his office, Chief Nate Buchannan is on the phone. "Cunningham, your freakin' idiot! Can't your people do anything right?"

"Simmer down, Nate. We'll take care of it." After a brief pause, Cunningham asks, "Did you get the package?"

"Yes, I got the package," Buchannan replies. The rage is still apparent in his voice.

"Where is it now?"

"In my desk drawer."

"That's a relief." After a moment, Cunningham asks, "Where are the witnesses now?"

"They think they're on their way to a safehouse on Canal Street."

"Un-huh. What kind of *security*…"

"Two of my men."

"I donno. That's pretty close to home…"

"You're the one who screwed it up in the first place so don't you dare criticize me."

"Get off my ass…" Cunningham snorts into the phone. Then after a brief pause, he softens, "Should I send Ricco and Tony to help?"

"Those two bumbling lunatics. They're the cause of all this grief in the first place, so don't bother," Buchannan sneers, and slams down the phone.

● ● ●

We're still walking behind the detectives who appear to be headed toward their car. Suddenly, Tag puts his arm around my waist and pulls me close. Leaning into me, he whispers, "Don't be alarmed, but my instincts tell me something isn't right. Just follow my lead…"

The part about not being alarmed alarms me and I stare at him. *My* instincts tell me to scream and run for dear life. The detectives are still a few paces in front of us, but before I can spring into action, Harris, jangles his car keys. Glancing over his shoulder, he says, "Our buggy is right over there," and points to the left.

Tag must have noticed the not this chick, I'm outta here look on my face. He places a restraining hand on my arm and holds me back. Before I can jerk lose from his grip he slides his arm around the back of my neck. Then, reaching across my face, he presses his hand over my mouth. He jerks me to the right, and sandwiching us between the rows of parked vehicles, he pushes me down into a crouched position. Seconds later, I hear Harris exclaim, "Here we are, folks…" then after a pause, he shouts, "HEY! Where'd they go?"

Tag puts his forefinger to his lips and I nod. Still crouching low, we duck-walk between the rows of cars. I can hear Harris and Crawford shouting and cursing as they search for us. We cautiously maneuver between the rows of cars putting distance between us and the detectives. When we're far enough from them, Tag stands and violently rocks a couple of the parked cars. The vibration sets off their alarms. Almost immediately, the noise excites sensors in several more cars and before long the parking lot is screaming with activated car alarms. We watch as people come swarming out of nearby buildings apparently curious as to what's going on in the parking lot.

Confident we won't be executed in the midst of so many witnesses we stand. Over the tops of the vehicles, Tag and I watch Harris and Crawford zero in on us. Harris shoots us a contemptuous smile and points his forefinger our direction. Simulating a pistol, he takes an imaginary shot at us. I shiver and my knees threaten to buckle so I lean against the nearest vehicle.

Tag, apparently noticing my distress, takes my arm. "You all right?" he asks.

"I think so…probably too much trauma for this country girl. My heart is thumping and my head is spinning."

Tag nods. "Know what ya mean. This is even too much trauma for this seasoned peace officer," he says with a forced smile. Looking around, he adds, "We've got to get transportation. I'm sure they've identified my SUV by now and probably know where I live. It's for certain we can't go back there."

"I'm so sorry I got you into this mess…" I say and fight back tears.

Tag puts his arm around my shoulder. "Hey, Tiger, remember I'm the one who took an oath to serve and protect—and besides I kinda like you." He then pulls me into a bear hug and I hug him back.

His embrace feels safe and warm and I'm reluctant to let go. However, I finally manage to say, "I'm feeling very exposed standing out here in the open. How 'bout taking a cab to Hertz and renting another car?"

"Probably our best option. Come on, we'll flag a cab down on the other side of the parking lot."

• • •

Once we get another rent-a-car, we head away from D.C. and I begin to relax.

"Since we apparently can't trust the cops, where do we go from here?" I query.

"I don't know yet…but I'm working on it," Tag says and then he adds, "You like Chinese?"

I'm amazed. "How can you think of eating at a time like this?"

"Because…I'm hungry."

I shake my head. "Not sure I can eat. All this cops and robbers stuff has had an adverse impact on me. But, to answer your question, yes, I do like Chinese!"

Tag reaches over and pats my hand, saying, "By the way, Meg, our forefathers would've been very proud of the way you handled yourself today. I know I am!"

I smile at his comment remembering our lunch at the *Founding Fathers* and my vow to imitate their spirit and patriotism. *How many light years ago was that?* I'm beginning to think I'm more of a chicken heart than a brave heart.

Tag interrupts my self-recrimination. "I know the perfect place. It's secluded and the food is terrific."

• • •

I've always been intrigued by the Chinese culture, architecture and customs. Tag's choice, *The Forbidden City*, does not disappoint. The restaurant is resplendent with oriental appointments and Chinese art and I'm grateful for the distraction but still can't help wondering how safe we really are.

The maître d' escorts us to a table, and handing us menus, he says, "Your server will be with you momentarily."

We thank him and he retreats. Still ogling the interior, I say, "I could stay here forever."

Tag takes a look around and then back at me. "Tell ya what, Tiger, when we get the bad boys behind bars, we'll take that famous slow boat to China on our honeymoon and you can experience it firsthand."

When he says *honeymoon*, I don't know if he's teasing or not. I reply, "I accept. That's the best offer I've had since Jimmy what's-his-name, my first grade heart throb, kissed me on Valentine's Day."

• • •

Buchannan's face was red with rage and the veins were bulging in his neck when Harris and Crawford confessed to losing the witnesses. Behind the chief's closed office door, the two detectives cringed in their chairs. They were probably fearing, or maybe even hoping, the chief was having a heart attack.

"You two incompetent fools are worse than Ricco and Tony! How in hell's name did our targets get away?" When Harris started to explain, Buchannan held up a restraining hand. "Never mind! Just never mind! Whatever your excuse, I don't want to hear it! Now get your ugly asses out of here before I...before I..." he stammers as he points a shaky finger toward the door.

The detectives clamor over each other in their rush to get out of the chief's office. Once out in the corridor, Harris exclaims, "I don't like the way the chief talks to us."

"Nor do I but we have no choice," Crawford replies.

Looking back toward the chief's office, Harris says, "Guess you're right. Wanna grab a brew before we knock off?"

Crawford looks at Harris, *He's like the brother I never had.* "Hell, yes," he says, as they walk toward the parking lot. "I'm buying." *Maybe someday I can even the score and repay the chief the favor.*

• • •

Buchannan immediately phones Cunningham and explains the situation. "I've initiated an APB for their arrest…"

"On what charge?" Cunningham demands.

"For now, escape. But I'll think of something more serious when we get 'em in custody. It'd be nice if they were killed trying to escape again."

As soon as he ends his call to Cunningham, Buchannan instructs his secretary to bring him the Marcella Hernandez' murder file. Reading through the reports, it dawns on him the two pesky witnesses could be charged with the Hernandez' murder. The reports listed a witness, Irene Westermeyer, who lived across the street from the Ratcliff's. Westermeyer stated, on the day of the murder, she saw a dark, late model SUV drive slowly down the street, turn around in the cul-de-sac and drive slowly back to the senator's residence parking in the driveway. Westermeyer said she was unable to see the license number. She said she saw a man and a woman in the vehicle. The man went to the door. Westermeyer said she was unable to clearly see the couple because it was raining so hard but she could see the woman had long, black hair. She said the man had his collar turned up and his head ducked against the rain when he went to the door so she didn't get a look at his face.

When asked if she saw anything else suspicious, Westermeyer said her attention was directed back to the television she had been watching—her favorite game show was just starting and she ceased looking out of the window.

• • •

Chin, Meg and Tag's waiter, appeared and took their order. He was back almost immediately with egg drop soup and salad. After refilling their water glasses, he returned to the kitchen to pick up the rest of the order. While Chin waited for the cook to put the finishing touches on the dishes, he paused before the small television set on the counter in the kitchen. Wong, the cook was obsessed with watching the news and constantly kept the set turned to the news channel. The beeping and the words flashing across the screen caught Chin's eye. ATTENTION — ALERT — ATTENTION! The screen suddenly flashed pictures of Megan Duval and Britt Taggert. An announcer off-screen was saying, "…Britt Taggert and Megan Duval are wanted in connection with the death of Marcella Hernandez, Senator Mitchell Radcliff's maid, who was tortured and murdered at the Senator's home two days ago."

The announcer continued, "Suspect Megan Duval's date of birth is August 28, 1993. She is described as being five feet seven inches tall, weighing one hundred thirty pounds with blond hair and blue eyes. Suspect Britt Taggert's date of birth is March 25, 1987. He is described as being six feet two inches tall, weighing one hundred eighty pounds with brown hair and brown eyes. Authorities warn that the couple is probably armed and dangerous. If you have any information regarding the pair, please contact the Washington D.C. Police Department. We have been advised that a two thousand dollar reward has been posted by Crime Stoppers for information leading to the arrest of Duval and Taggert."

An astonished Chin staggered against the kitchen counter when he recognized Meg and Tag. After a few seconds he regained his composure and went to the round window in the swinging door that separated the kitchen from the dining room. Taking another look at the couple, he gasped when he confirmed his suspicions—they were the individuals wanted by the police—and worth two thousand dollars!

"Order up!" Wong calls and looks in Chin's direction. Apparently, seeing the astonished look on Chin's face, he asks, "You okay, fú wú yuàn?"

Chin doesn't answer. Instead he jerks off his apron, tosses it on the counter, and heads for the owner's office. The only telephone in the restaurant was in the owner's office and Chin wasted no time dialing 911. Wong, with his gaze still focused on Chin, shrugs and delivers the dinner to Tag and Meg himself. Tag looks up when Wong approaches and then leans out of the booth looking around expecting to see Chin. Wong, apparently noticing Tag's concern, says, "Chin on break. I serve."

As soon as Wong departs, I ask, "Is something wrong?"

"Naw, just paranoid I guess." Then gesturing to the mound of food on each of their plates, Tag says, "Eat up, we've got a long way to go."

· · ·

Not long into our dinner *The Forbidden City* erupts into chaos. The restaurant is suddenly filled with policemen including a SWAT team rigged out in full gear. I'm stunned and sit frozen staring at the clamor the interruption created. When one of the officers demands, "Everyone stay where you are and keep your hands on the table," I look toward the entrance. Chin is standing beside one of the SWAT officers pointing in our direction.

Tag apparently notices it, too. "Easy, Meg…"

We're suddenly surrounded. Tag is yanked from the booth and his pistol is ripped from the holster on his belt. With his hands behind his back, he's placed in handcuffs. I, too, am pulled from the booth but not treated as roughly as Tag. However, my arms begin to ache when my hands are also cuffed behind my back. I watch as the officers empty the contents of my purse out on the table and sort through them. The officer in charge informs us we're being arrested for the murder of Marcella Hernandez. I grow lightheaded. *How can that be?* I look at Tag and he appears to be just as shaken as I am. We're forcibly ushered from the restaurant, separated and each of us is shoved into the backseat of a police cruiser.

• • •

The next time I see Tag is at our first court appearance. When booked, our personal belongings were confiscated and our clothes were exchanged for orange jail garb. We're now jammed together in a holding area with all the other overnight arrests. We're closely supervised by sheriff's deputies and not allowed to speak to each other. When the judge calls our case, Tag and I are escorted into the courtroom together since our cases have been joined.

The presiding judge appears to be absorbed in a file on her desk and doesn't look up during all the comings and goings taking place in her courtroom. Once we're seated and the deputy retreats, the judge removes a document from the file, clears her throat and reads the complaint filed against us. Each of us is charged with first degree murder and our individual bond is set at $1,000,000. The whole process is surreal and everything happens so fast, I feel as though I'm trudging through a nightmare.

Tag and I are then advised of our rights. When asked if we are indigent and will be requesting a court appointed attorney, we both answer in the negative and state we will be hiring private counsel.

At the conclusion of our advisement, we're taken back to the holding area to wait for the other overnight arrests to be advised. Though we don't speak to each other, Tag flashes a broad smile. Needless to say it's reassuring and I smile back. When the last of the inmates are advised, we're herded back to the Fairfax County Jail.

Alone in my cell, I'm feeling more isolated than ever. I wonder what Tag's thinking and wish I could talk to him. Not being able to afford to post a million dollar bond or hire a bondsman, I'm resigned to remain in jail. Since I have enough funds in savings to hire an attorney, I telephone Lincoln Turnbull, an attorney who at one time worked for the Department of Justice. He agreed to represent me. Tag hired Dalton Betcher, a former federal prosecutor.

• • •

The morning after my advisement hearing, Lincoln pays me a visit. We meet in one of the interrogation rooms in the detention facility and as we shake hands, he says, "Just call me Link. May I refer to you as Meg?"

"Yes, of course. Have you talked to Tag?" I ask.

"Tag?"

"Yes, Britt Taggert…"

"Oh, of course, your codefendant. No, at this stage it wouldn't be ethical for me to interview him. I will meet later with him and his attorney, and likewise, his attorney will meet with the two of us as we prepare for trial."

When Link says *trial*, I wilt. *Is this really happening? Or is all this just a nightmare?*

Link apparently doesn't notice my anxiety. His attention is directed to the file he places on the table between us. He opens the file and methodically sorts through the paperwork, rearranging some of the pages. "I have the discovery documents provided by the prosecuting attorney's office," he says. He takes them from the file, and as he hands them to me, we go over them one-by-one. The contents of the report are slanted in order to place Tag and me in a bad light and misstate the crucial facts concerning when and how the envelope with the note and ten thousand dollars ended up in Buchannan's hands. When I point that out to Link, he squints and stares at me. "Maybe you should start at the beginning," he says and removes a yellow legal pad from his valise.

I nod and am eager to get my story out. "To begin with, and what the prosecuting attorney probably has no way of knowing, is that my best friend, Jessica Stanton, was a pickpocket. She lifted an envelope from some guy in the mall four days ago."

Link looks up from the file and raises his brows, "A pickpocket?"

"Yes, that's how she put herself through college," I say. I assume as soon as my story is out I'll be vindicated and returned to a normal life so I quickly move on. "After lifting the envelope and determining its contents, Jess said she felt like she was in a compromising situation. She confided in me that she thought she was being stalked by her victim but that she didn't know how he tagged her. We had lunch the day after she lifted the envelope and she was extremely nervous. She kept looking around and even stuttered when she spoke. That behavior was out of character for Jess—she was always cool, calm and collected so I knew she wasn't kidding."

Link is taking notes as fast as I talk. He pauses and asks, "Does all of this have anything to do with the Hernandez murder?"

"Yes. I'm getting there…"

"Okay. Go on. Did Jess tell you what was in the envelope?"

"No. I found out later. There was a handwritten note and ten thousand dollars."

"If Jess didn't tell you, how'd you find out?"

"Well, Jess called me late the same night after we had lunch. She seemed to be in a panic and asked me to meet her at her place. I dropped everything and rushed to her apartment. When I got there, I found her dead body. I became hysterical and my screams probably woke the entire building. The neighbors called the cops." Recalling the ordeal, I dissolve in tears. *Poor Jess...*

"I see," Link says, and hands me his handkerchief. "Is that when you found the envelope with the note and the money?"

Still sniffling, I manage to say, "No. Jess apparently dropped it in the mail to me the same day she was killed. When I got home from the police station, I found it in a stack of mail I had dumped on my coffee table when I got home from work. I received the panic call from Jess before I sorted through the mail. After I was interviewed, the police escorted me home and went through my apartment to make sure I was safe. It was only after they left that I found the envelope."

"Okay, then what?"

"As soon as I saw the envelope I knew what it was. It was addressed to me in Jess' handwriting. When I opened it and discovered the contents, I surmised that was what got Jess killed. To make a long story short, as I paced the floor trying to decide what to do with the information now in my possession, I peeked out of my bedroom window. That's when I noticed a man standing in the shadows of a doorway across the street from my place. My instincts told me I was in danger so I threw some things in my overnight bag, including the envelope, and slipped out the back entrance of the apartment house. I took a cab to the CIA building thinking I'd be safe there," I almost laugh when I add, "I found myself in more danger there than I would've been out on the street."

Still scribbling, Link asks, "How's that?"

"After entering the building, I went to my boss' office. I was exhausted and fell asleep on the sofa. Sometime later I was awakened when I overheard my boss talking to someone on the phone. They were discussing the incident and Jess' murder. It was then I realized my boss, Special Agent Steve Cunningham, was in it up to his eyeballs. I had seen several oil exploration contracts on his desk a couple of weeks before and with Ratcliff expected to change his vote, Steve stood to lose a great deal of money. Lucky for me it was dark in his office and he didn't see me. During his phone conversation, he exploded in a fit of rage, slammed the phone down and rushed out of the office. As soon as he left I ran and hid waiting for the chance to make my escape."

Link looks up from his writing. "You're doing just fine. What happened then?"

"I commandeered one of the CIA cruisers in the driveway. Apparently, in their haste to come to the aid of their commander, the responding agents left the keys in the ignition and engine running. I hopped in and tore outta there busting through the closed entrance gate."

Link is smiling as he hands me a bottle of water. "Wish I could've seen that," he says. I return his smile remembering Steve standing on the steps waving his arms frantically in the air. I take a sip of water. It feels good to get my story out.

"Go on," Link coaxes.

"Well, I detected I was being followed but couldn't figure out how they knew where I was all the time. Several times I just barely dodged a bullet. It was quite by accident that I discovered a tracking device on the flap of the manila envelope. Realizing that's how my stalkers tracked me, I stuck the device on Moochy in a drive-in parking lot…"

"Moochy?"

"Yes, the cat that befriended me and my sausage McMuffin."

Now, Link laughs out loud but doesn't look up from his note taking. As he continues writing, he remarks, "All we need now is for PETA to come breathing down our necks."

I break into a grin when I think about Watson and Samuels following Moochy—right to the dumpster. "That's how I was able to shake my tail. Poor kitty, hope he survived. Tag, Britt Taggert, that is, my codefendant and the state patrolman who stopped me for speeding outside of D.C. I told him what I just related to you and he's been helping me ever since.

"Tag didn't kill Marcella Hernandez. In fact, we were there to warn the senator of the impending danger to his life. Neither of us entered the senator's residence and only Tag went to the door. Shortly after we left the Ratcliff estate, I noticed a suspicious looking car turn onto the same street and am certain the occupants were a couple agents I knew from working at the CIA, Eric Watson and Kenneth Samuels. The car looked very much like the one that had been chasing me all over the place.

"The witness is correct. We did drive past the senator's home intending to contact him and warn him of the imminent danger from the hitmen. We parked in the driveway, and as I stated, Tag went to the door and was told by the maid who answered that she didn't know where the senator was or how to contact him, so we left.

"Tag said he was acquainted with Chief Buchannan. He said the two had met at a law enforcement seminar they had attended some years before. Tag thought Buchannan was a standup guy and would be able to help us. Instead, Buchannan was in on the assassination plot and the one who painted the targets on our backs and dispatched two of his detectives, Clayton Harris and Tyler Crawford, to kill us. When they failed, apparently the chief put out an APB for our arrest. And the rest is history!"

"My God! I see what you mean when you say they jerry-rigged the facts. If we can prove the Chief of Police and a high-ranking CIA agent were behind the murders... Do you have any witnesses who can corroborate your story?"

I take a few moments to ponder the question. "Sadly enough, no. The only witnesses I know of who could help us are Jessica and Ratcliff's maid, Marcella Hernandez. They both, of course, are now deceased."

The look on Link's face says it all. I get the feeling he thinks we're dead in the water. Bad choice of words considering how Marcella Hernandez died.

CHAPTER SEVEN

Go Fish...

Since Tag and I are both charged with the murder of Marcella Hernandez, our cases have been joined and we're scheduled to be tried together. Link's request for severance was summarily denied by Judge Goldstein. Link's afraid I'll be convicted because of my association with Tag. He explained the concept of guilt by association and the advantage of the two of us being tried separately—a benefit more for me than Tag. The upside is that by the two cases being joined I may help Tag's cause. Link said that if I'm convicted, the denial of our request bolsters my chance of reversal on appeal.

Our lawyers request a speedy trial, that is a trial within six months of the date of arraignment. The ensuing days are crammed with trial preparation. Link and I meet regularly with Tag and his attorney, Dalton Betcher. These meetings afford Tag and me a chance to communicate—for which I'm grateful. Our attorneys are sympathetic to our situation and give us a few minutes alone after each combined session. Tag appears to be holding up well—much better than me—well, on the surface anyway. I don't allow myself to think too far into the future. When we examine the evidence against us, it is difficult to be optimistic.

Although I'm somewhat familiar with legalese having worked for the CIA, I still have a lot to learn. Tag, of course, has made numerous court appearances as the arresting officer on his traffic cases so he's more in tune with the legal process and court proceedings than am I.

Our list of witnesses is pathetic compared to the prosecution's list. Link asks me to study the witnesses stacked against us. Other than forensic and technical witnesses, most of the others are ones involved in the murder investigation itself.

"Link," I say, "I don't see a friendly name on this list." Link follows as I trace the names with my forefinger. "Eric Watson and Kenneth Samuels are the two CIA agents who followed me for a couple of days—who no doubt had the intention of eliminating me.

"Detectives Tyler Crawford and Clayton Harris are the ones who tried to kill us in the parking lot the afternoon after we took the envelope containing the incriminating evidence to the police department. I'm sure the Chief of Police, Nate Buchannan, orchestrated that hit. I don't think there's a safe house on Canal Street and that that was just a ruse to set us up for the kill. If it wasn't for Tag's quick thinking, it would have worked.

"Then there's my CIA boss, Special Agent Steve Cunningham. I know for a fact he sent Agents Watson and Samuels to chase me down. I heard the phone call with my own ears."

I pause for a moment when I get to Senator Ratcliff's name. "The senator may well be the only person we can rely on."

Link nods and underlines Ratcliff's name. "I'll see about interviewing the senator," he says as he gathers his files into his valise. After Link leaves, I'm more depressed than ever. Going over the list with him convinces me that our chances of being exonerated are little to none.

●　●　●

Our attorneys have compiled a litany of motions. At our next meeting, they go over them with us. Dalton points out that the most important one is our motion for change of venue. The press had a heyday demonizing us and the newspapers were plastered with pictures of the *Killer Couple* accompanied by scathing articles detailing how, in the reporter's view, we murdered Hernandez. In the days leading up to trial, the press became even more relentless in their quest to see that justice was meted out to the *heartless bastards.*

• • •

CIA Agent Cunningham and Chief Buchannan sit across from each other in a dimly lit bar. It is mid-afternoon and the lunch crowd has dissipated and the five-o'clockers have yet to arrive.

"I'm painfully aware Watson and Samuels are *your* men. You can vouch for them all you want, but I still think they're a liability," Buchannan says to Cunningham.

"Wrong! They know better than to betray me," Cunningham sneers.

"Sure they do!" Buchannan says with scorn in his voice. "Use your head, Steve. They got carried away and needlessly killed those two women, Hernandez and that Jessica what's her name. If the DA put the screws to 'em and offered 'em a deal, they'd sing like canaries. After all, do you think the DA would settle for a couple of minnows when there are whales to be snagged?"

Cunningham, looking thoughtful, rubs the back of his neck.

After a few uncomfortable moments, Buchannan continues, "I can have a couple of my guys eliminate the Samuels slash Watson problem before some smart cop manages to put two and two together."

"Hold on, Nate! My agents—" Cunningham

hisses, but Buchannan cuts him off.

"Right! Your agents may as well have left their calling cards at the senator's place. Just how many assassins do you suppose use the waterboard technique? The waterboarding certainly ties the CIA to the murder. Besides, that nosy neighbor across the street may remember seeing Samuels and Watson at the senator's house that afternoon..."

Cunningham appears to be trying to control his anger as he swirls the ice around in his glass. He finally scoffs, "Then what? You gonna want to eliminate the nosy neighbor across the street along with Crawford and Harris? We can't just keep killing people..."

Buchannan, with fire in his eyes, slams his palm down on the table, "You hold on, Steve!"

The other customers in the bar stop what they were doing and look toward the two men who appear to be engaged in a heated argument. Apparently, when it's determined there isn't going to be a fist fight, the patrons return to their drinking and chatting.

Buchannan, looking sheepish, leans closer to Cunningham, and in a more subdued tone, says, "Let me refresh your memory. It was *your* people who got us into this jam in the first place. And I might add, those two bozos you call CIA agents couldn't find their way out of a paper bag. How is it they let this Megan person slip through their fingers time and time again? Even with a tracking device they managed to screw it up. Doesn't sound to me like they're too damn competent. I can guarantee Crawford and Harris can be trusted! They never question my authority and always find a way to get the job done!"

Cunningham, looking exasperated, relents, "Okay, okay. You win. Since your people are so competent and loyal, I'll let you handle the details. I'm washing my hands of this one…"

"Of course you are, you hypocrite!" And with that Buchannan stands and tosses a twenty dollar bill onto the table. "Watch your six," he sneers as he turns toward the exit.

Cunningham looks up, with anger apparent in his eyes. "That comment sounds more like a threat than a statement."

"Take it any way you want…"

• • •

Back at the office, Buchannan summons Crawford and Harris. "I've a very sensitive assignment for the two of you," he begins. The detectives sit rigid in their chairs—waiting. Buchannan continues, "There are two rogue CIA agents out there. They're the ones who killed

Stanton and Hernandez. Right now, they're loose cannons and need to be dealt with before they bring down the house of cards."

Crawford shifts in his chair. Glancing at Harris, he notices Harris appears to be uneasy as well. Crawford then directs his attention back at Buchannan, "You looking for a permanent solution…?"

"Yes," the chief answers, without hesitation.

Crawford nods. "And who are these loose cannons?"

"Eric Watson and Kenneth Samuels."

"Hey, we know those guys…" Crawford starts to protest, but is immediately silenced by the look on Buchannan's face.

A few awkward moments pass before Harris asks, "Time frame?"

"ASAP!"

• • •

Once out of the chief's office, Harris asks Crawford, "What'd you think?"

"Sounds as though Watson and Samuels have something big on the chief and his buddy, Cunningham, and they want them silenced."

"Yeah! Well, how 'bout us? After we do the job, who gets to silence us?" Harris mumbles.

"You make a good point. Maybe we can just

warn them…" Crawford offers.

"Don't think so. That would be signing our own death warrants."

● ● ●

The next day Crawford places a call to Watson. "A reliable source tipped us that there's going to be a big drug deal going down tonight. The snitch guarantees the kitty will be worth a couple of mil." Crawford holds his breath, hoping Watson will take the bait. When he gets no immediate response, he adds, "Me and Harris can't do it alone. If you and Samuels want a piece of the action, you know of course, we don't have to account for all of the contraband…"

After a few moments, Watson asks, "How 'bout the locals?"

"Why cut the pie in more pieces than we have to? I think the four of us can take 'em down…and get paid pretty well for our efforts, if you follow my drift," Crawford says.

"Hold on, let me talk to Samuels." A few minutes pass before Watson is back on the line. "When and where?"

Crawford gives Harris a thumbs up as he replies to Watson, "The junk yard on Lexington and Melrose. Meet us there around midnight. That'll give us enough time to set up an ambush."

"How many hostiles you expecting?" Watson asks.

"Snitch says four. Should be a piece of cake." After a brief pause, Crawford adds, "We'll be watching for you guys."

"Roger that."

• • •

As soon as Watson ends the call he dissolves into a coughing fit covering his mouth with his handkerchief. When the coughing subsides, he refolds the handkerchief and notices some blood spots. *What the hell?*

Samuels remarks, "What's wrong, Eric?"

"What do ya mean?" Watson asks.

"Your coughing fits—they're too violent, too frequent and just don't sound like you have a cold or allergies."

"Oh, that. Probably nothing—I'll get an appointment later this week and have the doc take a look."

• • •

The junk yard is dark, cold and damp from an earlier rain. Crawford and Harris, having previously arrived, are secluded behind some rusted out cars waiting for their prey. When they spot Watson and Samuels slowly driving through the heaps of scrap metal, they hunker down and draw their weapons.

They watch as Watson and Samuels come to a stop and slowly exit their vehicle.

When their prey is far enough from their vehicle, Harris carefully draws a bead on Watson's head. However, before he can get a shot off Watson bends over, erupting in a bout of coughing. Startled by the noise, Harris jerks his hand up and the shot goes wild. When Samuels hears the shot, he immediately hits the dirt. Reaching up, he grabs Watson by the forearm and jerks him down. Crouching, Samuels looks around for a better place to hide. When he notices a pile of scrap directly to their right, he nudges Watson and points. Watson nods.

"On the count of three," Samuels whispers. Watson nods again. When Samuels says, "One, two, three, go!" they break cover, scrambling to a spot behind the heap of metal. Once out of sight, they hunker down gasping for air.

Once they've caught their breath and feel more secure, Watson shouts, "Crawford! Is that you?"

By way of answer, Crawford and Harris unload their service revolvers into the scrap heap where it appears Watson and Samuels are hiding. Their challenge is returned by a hail of bullets from the other side. Seconds into the gun battle, Samuels groans and collapses against Watson.

"Ken, Ken," Watson whispers but Samuels does

not respond. Watson feels for a pulse but doesn't find one. He then closes Samuels' eyes and wipes a tear from his own. *Back stabbing, rotten bastards...*

Watson hunkers down and waits. As minutes pass without movement from the other side, Watson decides to use Samuels' body as a decoy to ascertain if the opposition is still alive. He pulls the limp body into a sitting position, and with his hand supporting the back of Samuels' head, Watson wobbles Samuels' head around hoping to bait his nemeses into firing at them if they're still alive. When nothing happens, Watson concludes Crawford and Harris are probably dead or seriously wounded.

Being careful to avoid sharp protrusions, Watson climbs from his hiding place and ducks between piles of junk, making his way to where he believes Crawford and Harris are secluded. The headlights on the CIA vehicle are still on thus enabling Watson to easily locate the bodies. He finds them both dead.

• • •

When Buchannan receives word that his two detectives, as well as CIA Agent Samuels, were killed in the ambush he and Cunningham orchestrated, he's relieved to have at least three of them silenced. However, one of the CIA agents, Eric Watson, is still alive—and probably now perceives he has a score to settle. Buchannan concludes that Watson is smart enough to figure out the alleged drug deal was a setup in order to eliminate him and Samuels because of the Hernandez murder.

Buchannan, in a rage, grabs his phone and dials Cunningham's inside line.

"Yeah!" Cunningham answers and Buchannan immediately barks in a loud voice, "Your *competent* employees sure blew that one!"

"Easy, Nate…"

"Easy, my ass! Do you realize the position we're now in?"

"Yes…" Cunningham replies.

"Yes? Is that all you can say. One of *your* men is now rogue and can put us away for life."

"I know that…"

"Well, what are you going to do about it?" Buchannan demands.

"ME? How about you?" Cunningham shouts back, pounding his desk with his fist. "Your two crack detectives blew it! And by the way, you have as much skin in the game as I do!" After a brief pause, Cunningham grows calm and continues, "At this point it doesn't matter whose fault it was, we've got to come up with a solution before we're all behind bars."

"Do you think you're the only one with a brain?

I've already started the process. I've got a couple of my detectives watching Watson's place and have placed an APB out on him and his vehicle."

Cunningham is not accustomed to being insulted and wants to rip Buchannan's heart out. However, because of the circumstances, he reins in his temper and says, "That's a good start." After a brief silence, he adds, "Anyway, keep me posted on your progress."

"Roger that," Buchannan answers and slams the phone down.

• • •

Watson, because of his wanted status, just dropped out of sight. His coughing spells grew more frequent and violent after Samuels was killed. Laying low in a cheap motel, Watson decides to make a doctor's appointment. He's sitting on the examination table buttoning his shirt when his doctor, Bryan Haslip, enters the room.

"What's the story, doc?" Watson asks, hopeful expectation evident in his voice.

"Sorry, Eric, bad news," Dr. Haslip replies and watches Watson sag as though the wind had been knocked out of his sails.

"Just give it to me straight…"

Haslip places an x-ray onto the screen adjacent to the examination table and turns the light on. With his forefinger, he traces a spot on the screen. "X-rays reveal you have stage four lung cancer. Sorry, Eric, it's inoperable."

Although stunned by the sudden revelation of a death sentence, Watson maintains his composure, and after a brief pause, asks, "How long do I have?"

"Six, eight weeks—give or take…"

Pulling on his shoes, Watson looks up at the doctor, "Will it be painful?"

"When it gets to that stage, I'll hospitalize you and put you on a morphine drip. That will ease the pain. Other than that…"

Watson nods again. "Will I be in control of my faculties?"

"For the most part, yes."

• • •

Watson hadn't had contact with anyone since the shootout and was careful to avoid familiar haunts. He felt relatively safe in the motel room and was sure none of his friends or fellow officers knew where he was.

The media coverage on Samuels' funeral was extensive and multiple CIA and other law enforcement personnel from near and far were expected to attend to pay their respects and bid farewell to their fallen comrade. The day of the funeral Watson donned a disguise and took a taxi to the cemetery. It was a cold, wet day and the slight breeze made it seem even colder than the thermometer read. Watson bundled up in a heavy coat and placed a wool scarf around his neck so that it obstructed most of his face. Shivering, he positioned himself on the fringe of the mourners keeping a distance from the locals so as not to be recognized. The burial service was well attended with what he guessed to be more than 100 peace officers along with civilian and military personnel.

After the service, Watson hung back in the shadow of a large oak tree. When the crowd had dissipated, he approached Samuels' grave and went down on one knee. *I'll be joining you in a few weeks, Ken, but before I go, I'll even the score—for the both of us. Until we meet again, rest in peace.* Then rising, he snapped a smart salute, turned and walked away.

CHAPTER EIGHT

Truth or Dare...

In the ensuing days, Watson followed the *Killer Couple's* press coverage with intense interest. The media had a field day with the label *Killer Couple* and it had by now become a household description. Watson speculated that the media's use of the label could possibly result in the defense obtaining a change of venue because of its prejudicial connotation.

NOT GUILTY PLEAS ENTERED BY KILLER COUPLE
TRIAL SET FOR EARLY MAY.

The accused, Megan Duval and Britt Taggert, appeared with their attorneys Lincoln Turnbull and Dalton Betcher, respectively, for their formal arraignment before District Judge Harden Goldstein. Both defendants entered pleas of not guilty and both requested a jury trial.

The defense was granted thirty days to file defense motions; the prosecution, represented by District Attorney Fletcher Schumacher, was granted fifteen days to respond. A motions hearing is scheduled for a four-hour block of time beginning at 8:00 a.m. on March 17. Turnbull and Betcher stated that the defense expected to file three motions: Motion for Change of Venue; Motion to Suppress Evidence and Motion to Suppress Eyewitness Testimony.

The defense announced they would waive speedy trial allowing the trial to commence outside the six-month period measured from the date of plea. Because of the severity of the charge and the complexity of the case, four weeks have been set aside for the jury trial. Jury selection is scheduled to begin at 8:00 a.m. on May 8.

• • •

At our motions hearing, Link puts up a valiant argument in defense of our motion for change of place of trial. "The defendants have already been tried and convicted by the media," he states. "Because of the massive and pervasive prejudicial pretrial publicity, the defendants cannot receive a fair trial as guaranteed by the Sixth Amendment to the United States Constitution—at least not in Fairfax County, Virginia," he continues. "In the interests of justice, Your Honor, the trial must be moved to a jurisdiction where the jury pool has not been exposed to or tainted by all the hype and prejudicial pretrial publicity and where the defendants can receive a fair trial."

I watch Judge Goldstein's face. It's apparent he can't wait until Link is seated to rule on the motion. Needless to say, it was summarily denied.

The judge reasoned that, because the victim was employed by a high-profile individual, namely Senator Ratcliff, and that the senator's vote on the pending coal phase-out bill was a topic of intense national concern, newspapers and television stations across the country had an ongoing interest in reporting the story. He concluded by stating, "The idea that ignorance of national news qualifies one to be an impartial juror is ludicrous. The defense's assertion that it would most likely be impossible to find twelve potential jurors anywhere in the state who were not exposed to the story flies in the face of reason…"

As soon as Link takes his seat, Dalton goes to the podium and addresses the Motion to Suppress Eyewitness Testimony. He argues that Irene Westermeyer stated she didn't get a good look at the occupants of the vehicle in question. "It's apparent her attention was divided between a program she was watching on television and what was happening at Senator Ratcliff's residence across the street from where she lived. Westermeyer stated, on the day of the murder, she saw a dark, late model, SUV drive slowly down the street, turn around in the cul-de-sac and drive slowly back to the Senator's residence parking in the driveway. She also stated she was unable to see the license number, and that she saw what appeared to be a man and woman in the vehicle. The man went to the door. Westermeyer said she was unable to clearly see the couple because it was raining so hard."

Dalton continues to argue, "Mr. Taggert's automobile is not an uncommon make, model or color, and because of the weather conditions, the witness herself admits it was difficult if indeed not impossible to clearly see the occupants."

Dalton also argued the Motion to Suppress Evidence. "The note and ten thousand dollars were turned over to the authorities by the defendants a long time prior to their arrest in an effort to stymie an assassination attempt on United States Senator Mitchell Ratcliff and other than being good citizens there's no other nexus to the murder of Marcella Hernandez."

Although our attorneys prepared us for the possibility that Judge Goldstein would deny our motions, Tag and I sit in silence beside our lawyers at the defense table stunned when the judge summarily denies all three—especially our motion for change of venue. Even with the deaths and thus unavailability of three key prosecution witnesses, things are looking bleaker by the minute. Hope is fading fast!

• • •

Although Eric Watson was listed as a prosecution witness, his disappearance precluded him from having been served with a subpoena to testify. Watson was aware of the facts of the case, and as he watched the trial unfold on the television screen in his motel room, he marveled at how Buchannan and Cunningham were able to manipulate the reports to completely distort the truth. He concluded that with his disappearance and the deaths of the other three main prosecution witnesses, Tyler Crawford, Clayton Harris and Kenneth Samuels, the outcome of the trial was a tossup. However, it was obvious the needle edged more in the direction of the prosecution than the defense. The eyewitness, Irene Westermeyer, was the linchpin the prosecution was now hanging their hats on. If the jury believed Westermeyer was able to see enough from her living room window to be a credible witness, then game over for the defense.

• • •

On the day of trial, as soon as the court dispenses with the preliminaries and a jury is seated, Judge Goldstein asks Schumacher if the people are ready to proceed with the prosecution's case in chief.

"We are, Your Honor," Schumacher replies. "Will the court allow me a minute to explain to the jury why some of our witnesses are *unavailable* to testify?"

Judge Goldstein, looks perplexed for a moment. Then, obviously realizing what Schumacher is referring to, says, "Bailiff, please remove the jury while the court addresses this issue."

Schumacher starts to say something but the judge holds up a restraining hand. Once the jury has been taken out, Judge Goldstein replies, "The court understands your predicament, Mr. Schumacher. However, I'm assuming you have no depositions from the three deceased witnesses, only their police reports."

"That's correct, Your Honor."

"Then you've been a prosecutor long enough to know, even live witnesses are not allowed to testify by reading from their reports—only refer to them if need be during questioning. In this case, having another read the reports into evidence is tantamount to hearsay."

Schumacher holds up a hand, "May I explain

my position?"

"Briefly," the judge grudgingly relents.

"Thank you, Your Honor. The matter before the court deals with extremely unusual circumstances. I don't recall another case in recent history where three of the key witnesses were killed before trial."

The judge cuts Schumacher off midsentence. "Mr. Schumacher, I, myself, am a historian. If I may take you back to the infamous mobster trials of the '30s, you may recall that it was not unusual for witnesses to die, disappear or otherwise be *unavailable* to testify at trial. Be that as it may, the trials proceeded without them or their testimony unless they were deposed before their deaths—or whatever."

"Yes, but…" Schumacher persists.

"Mr. Schumacher, I'm sure you understand that, as a sworn judge of the state court, it is my obligation to follow the law. I cannot make exceptions to accommodate your circumstances." Goldstein pauses momentarily before continuing, "The defendants are each charged with a capital offense, that's life in prison or the death penalty. I will not jeopardize their constitutional rights to afford the prosecution a more favorable position."

The judge removes his glasses and rubs the bridge of his nose while we all wait on pins and needles. Seconds drag past and we watch as he pours water from a pitcher into a glass on his desk. After taking a drink, he continues, "Due to the fact that the defense will not have the opportunity to cross-examine your witnesses, the court rules that, in the interests of justice and to avoid undue prejudice or the likelihood thereof, your request is hereby denied."

I turn slightly and glance at Buchannan and Cunningham who are present in court. It's apparent they're not happy with the ruling. And the shocked look on Schumacher's face indicates that he is in disbelief that the court would not allow him to tell the jury that three of his key witnesses were recently killed in an ambush. Schumacher finally manages to say, "But, Your Honor…"

Judge Goldstein again holds up a restraining hand, "Mr. Schumacher, I've ruled on your motion! If there's nothing else to address, we'll continue."

"Yes, sir," Schumacher mutters, quite obviously shaken by the reprimand and the adverse ruling. Now he has to instantly reinvent his presentation to exclude the testimony of the deceased witnesses, Crawford, Harris and Samuels.

Pointing to the bailiff, the judge orders, "Bring the jury back in."

• • •

To his credit, Schumacher, a seasoned prosecutor, is able to roll with the punches. He soon regains his momentum, and clearing his throat, begins. "Ladies and gentlemen of the jury, we thank you for giving your time to serve as jurors in the case of *People of the State of Virginia v. Megan Duval and Britt Taggert.* The codefendants are charged with first degree murder. The people will show that the defendants had the means, motive and opportunity to kill Marcella Hernandez. The people will also show that the aforementioned victim, a maid for Senator Mitchell Ratcliff, was alone at the residence on the afternoon of November 4, 2017, when the defendants arrived at the senator's home and engaged the victim in conversation.

"An eyewitness, Irene Westermeyer, who lives across the street from the Ratcliffs, will testify that, on the day of the murder, she saw a dark, late model SUV drive slowly down the street, turn around in the cul-de-sac and drive slowly back to the senator's residence parking in the driveway. Westermeyer will also testify that she was unable to see the license number but that she saw a man and woman in the vehicle. The man went to the door. Westermeyer will testify that she was unable to clearly see the couple because of the heavy downpour but could see that the woman resembled Ms. Duval. She will testify that the man had his head ducked, apparently against the rain, when he went to the door so she didn't get a good look at his face. She, however, described him as a tall, well-built man matching the description of Mr. Taggert.

"Basically, the prosecution will unravel the mystery even though the majority of the people's witnesses were…"

Link is on his feet. "Objection!"

"On what grounds?" Judge Goldstein asks.

"Mr. Schumacher is attempting to garner sympathy, bias and prejudice in favor of the people's case and appears to be getting into an area previously ruled on by the court."

I notice the jurors looking perplexed not knowing, of course, that three key witnesses of the prosecution had been killed in an ambush.

"Objection sustained."

Schumacher is unabashed. He was apparently expecting the ruling so he proceeds to outline the prosecution's case in chief:

"The prosecution will be presenting an envelope marked People's Exhibit A which contains a note which reads, 'Your target must be eliminated before the final Senate vote on Tuesday. If you screw this up, you may be the one in the crosshairs. You know how to contact me when the job is done.' Inside the envelope is also ten thousand dollars in cash. D.C. Metropolitan Police Chief Nate Buchannan will testify the envelope with its contents was in the possession of the defendants at the time of their arrest."

Astonished at the blatant lie, I look at Link but before I can say anything, both Link and Dalton are on their feet objecting.

"The court can only hear one person at a time," Judge Goldstein scolds.

Dalton gestures to Link to proceed first.

Link nods and begins: "Your Honor, Ms. Duval objects on the grounds that the envelope with its contents were *provided* by her and Mr. Taggert to Chief Buchannan hours before their arrest, not *taken* from them incident to an arrest, as insinuated by the prosecution. We move that the offending word be stricken and that Mr. Schumacher be instructed not to misstate the evidence." Link then looks back over his shoulder, nods to Dalton and then sits down.

Dalton rises from his chair, "We make the same objection and request in behalf of Mr. Taggert," he says.

Judge Goldstein takes only a moment to reflect on his ruling. "The jury is instructed that statements of the attorneys are not evidence. Since opening statements are in essence offers of proof, the objections are denied. The jury will have the opportunity later to determine whether the attorneys proved what they promised to prove." Then gesturing toward the prosecutor, the judge says, "You may proceed, Mr. Schumacher."

Schumacher continues, "Several days after receiving the envelope with the note and ten thousand dollars, the D.C. Metropolitan Police Department received a call that a possibly armed gunman was apprehended in the balcony of the Senate Chambers after causing a scene and spectators and senators alike to run for cover. The suspect, of course, was none other than Britt Taggert, the individual seated next to his attorney, Dalton Betcher." With that, Schumacher points at Britt.

After a brief pause, Schumacher says, "Britt Taggert at that time was a Virginia State Trooper. Ms. Duval, who is seated here in court next to her attorney, Lincoln Turnbull, and a confederate of Mr. Taggert's, was also present at the time of the disruption in the United States Senate. It was the two of them who were in possession of the envelope with the note and the ten thousand dollars. The evidence will show that Ms. Duval was an employee of the CIA at the time of her arrest and at the time Senator Ratcliff's maid, the victim in this case, was brutally murdered."

The few jurors who were not glaring at me before now do so. Schumacher's opening statement was having its intended effect. I sink lower into my chair as Schumacher continues to cast his spell over the jury. They closely watch his every move as he continues, "Motive? Well, quite obviously, and the evidence will support the theory that their motive was the lure of easy money. The defendants were both in a position of public trust and had the means, motive and opportunity to execute the assassination of Senator Ratcliff. Their scheme, however, was foiled when they discovered their target was not at home—they then had to do away with Marcella Hernandez, a witness who could identify them."

Schumacher then shakes his head in contrived disgust before concluding, "The evidence in this case is overwhelming and in seeking justice, we will be asking at the conclusion of the case for you to return a guilty verdict against both defendants—not because we are asking that you do so but because both are guilty of murder in the first degree."

• • •

During a much needed recess, we regroup in a conference room with our attorneys. It's obvious that Britt is as shaken as I am by the prosecution's opening remarks.

"We still have a long way to go so don't let

the prosecutor's version of events shake your confidence," Dalton says. "It's our turn to make opening statements and we can explain the allegations presented by the prosecutor."

Yep, and all we have to do is disprove them—but how? I'm despondent. There's no one in our corner and the evidence appears to be stacked against us. Recess is over and we're back in the courtroom and Dalton takes the lead.

"Ladies and gentlemen of the jury, my name is Dalton Betcher. I represent Britt Taggert, one of the defendants in this case. Although a defendant in an American courtroom is not required to testify or present evidence, we feel you're entitled to hear Britt Taggert's side of the story. Needless to say he will be called as a witness to proclaim his innocence."

Placing his forearms on the podium, Dalton leans toward the jury and says, "Come back with me to the night of November third of this past year. While on duty, Britt, Trooper Taggert that is, had occasion to stop a vehicle being driven by Megan Duval for speeding. Yes, the same Megan Duval who is seated at the defense table here along with her attorney, Lincoln Turnbull." Dalton gestures in my direction and I watch all eyes turn toward me. I feel myself flush with embarrassment at having been placed in this situation. Dalton continues.

"Upon stopping Ms. Duval and his subsequent investigation, Trooper Taggert concluded that there was an assassination plot to kill United States Senator Mitchell Ratcliff. In an effort to warn Senator Ratcliff of the impending plot, he, along with his codefendant, went to the senator's residence. That would have been on November fourth. Trooper Taggert spoke to the victim in this case, the senator's maid, Marcella Hernandez, at the front door of the senator's residence. There is no evidence indicating Trooper Taggert went inside of the house. Hernandez advised him that the senator was not in."

Schumacher is on his feet. "Objection, Your Honor, hearsay."

Turning to Dalton, Judge Goldstein says, "Mr. Betcher?"

"Your Honor, what the maid said will not be offered for the truth of the matter asserted—only to explain the defendants' actions thereafter."

"Very well," Judge Goldstein says, "the objection is overruled."

Dalton turns back to face the jury. "Not finding the senator at home," he continues, "and unable to schedule an appointment, the two defendants, realizing they were running out of time, came up with a fallback plan. At this point their only option was to try to warn the senator and stave off the assassination when the bill the senator was to consider—the highly controversial piece of legislation involving the coal phase-out bill —came before the Senate the next day for a vote.

"Trooper Taggert and Ms. Duval went to the U.S. Capitol Building and took up strategic positions across from each other, one on each side of the balcony. These positions allowed them not only to view their portion of the balcony, but to look across and see the other's side as well. Their hope, as I stated, was to thwart any assassination attempt on Senator Ratcliff.

"Before the Senate vote could be taken, Ms. Duval, from her position in the balcony, spotted one of the spectators she recognized as Eric Watson. Watson was a CIA agent she had seen numerous times at the CIA building where she worked. She had previously been stalked by Eric Watson and his partner, Kenneth Samuels, and she was in possession of information that Watson and Samuels were involved in the assassination plot.

"When Ms. Duval saw Watson in the Senate balcony, she pointed and shouted. Trooper Taggert sprang into action. The Senate erupted into chaos and during the melee, Trooper Taggert was mistaken for a would-be assassin. He was subdued by the

Senate security guards and taken into custody."

Collecting his notes, Dalton then says, "Trooper Taggert will testify that he had no motive to kill the senator's maid or to assassinate the senator and was in no way involved in Ms. Hernandez' murder. Not knowing who to trust, he will confess to having taken the law into his own hands to thwart the assassination. At the conclusion of the case you will be instructed that Britt Taggert doesn't have to prove anything—that it's incumbent upon the prosecution to prove his guilt beyond a reasonable doubt. If the evidence presented is as anticipated, we will have no hesitancy at the conclusion of the case in asking you to return a not guilty verdict."

As soon as Dalton takes his seat, Link is instructed to give the opening statement in my behalf. Link appears confident as he begins. Looking intently at the jury, he says, "My name is Lincoln Turnbull. I represent Megan Duval. Ms. Duval is a *magna cum laude* graduate from Willington-York University and spent her five-year career working for the CIA as an aid to CIA Senior Agent Steve Cunningham.

"On November third of last year, Ms. Duval stumbled upon a plot to assassinate United States Senator Mitchell Ratcliff. She determined the reason for the assassination was an attempt to prevent the passage of the coal phase-out bill in which Senator Ratcliff held the swing vote."

Link looks back at me before continuing, "Worse yet, she overheard a telephone conversation between her supervisor, Senior Agent Cunningham, and an unknown person discussing an assassination plot to eliminate Senator Ratcliff before he could cast his vote against the bill. Armed with that information and the envelope marked People's Exhibit A referred to by Mr. Schumacher containing the note he read to you and the ten thousand dollars, and no one to trust and time being of the essence, she headed back to Washington, D.C. In her rush to warn the senator, she was stopped by Trooper Taggert for exceeding the speed limit."

Link pauses, apparently to allow the jury time to absorb his comments. He walks back to the defense table and takes a drink of water. Now back at the podium, he continues, "When asked where she was headed in such a hurry, Ms. Duval, in a panic, blurted out her story involving the plot to assassinate Senator Ratcliff, her bosses' involvement in the plot and the envelope containing the note and currency. The evidence will show that the envelope with the note and currency was mailed to Ms. Duval by her ex-college roommate who was later found murdered execution style in her apartment. The evidence will further show that the envelope contained a hidden tracking device and Ms. Duval found herself being pursued by CIA Agents Eric Watson and Kenneth Samuels. After turning over the envelope and contents to D.C. Metropolitan Police Chief Nate Buchannan, someone she thought she could trust, she found herself along with Trooper Taggert being the target of not only the aforesaid CIA agents but the target of two detectives from the D.C. Metropolitan Police Department."

Pausing briefly to rearrange his notes on the podium, Link continues. "Ladies and gentlemen," he says with a grim expression, "like Trooper Taggert, not knowing who to trust and attempting to thwart an assassination attempt, Ms. Duval will testify that she embarked on a course of conduct she thought to be the only option available under the circumstances—one calculated to save the life of Senator Mitchell Ratcliff. She will categorically deny being part of the assassination plot or being involved in any way in the shocking death of the senator's maid, Marcella Hernandez. At the close of all the evidence, we'll be asking you to return a not guilty verdict."

The eyes of the jurors follow Link as he returns to his seat. Their expressions are also grim. Some tilt their heads; others shake their heads; and still others fold their arms across their chests. "We've got them thinking," Link whispers to me, "Appears they're starting to realize there's another side to the story."

• • •

The procession of witnesses follows the usual murder prosecution script. It starts with the responding officers and crime scene investigators; the county coroner; the pathologist who performed the autopsy; the lab technicians who testified as to the results of their testing; and the probable cause for arresting Tag and me.

The prosecution's case is based on the eyewitness account of Irene Westermeyer who states she saw a man and woman at Senator Ratcliff's home matching Tag's and my descriptions at the time of the murder of the named victim, Marcella Hernandez. The prosecution is bolstered by the testimony of D.C. Metropolitan Police Chief Nate Buchannan's false account of having *confiscated* the envelope containing the note and ten thousand dollars from us at the time of our arrest; Tag's arrest at the U.S. Senate; and me trying to frame my boss, Steve Cunningham in the *false plot* to assassinate Senator Ratcliff; and in the event of an assassination, to shift the blame onto him.

● ● ●

The stinging cross-examination of the prosecution's witnesses conducted by Dalton and Link start with the crime scene investigators.

Dalton leads off:

"Detective Zoren, you say you and Detective Parker combed the murder scene for clues as to who may have murdered Ms. Hernandez. Correct?"

"Yes."

Dalton looks up from his notes and asks, "I assume the two of you being seasoned crime scene investigators were thorough in the attempted collection and preservation of such things as fingerprints, foot prints and DNA samples?"

"Absolutely."

Dalton smiles and says, "So, this wasn't your first rodeo?"

"No," Zoren replies and smiles back at Dalton.

"In your report, you indicate that Mrs. Hernandez' body was found submerged in a bathtub filled with water. Correct?"

"Yes."

"And that she was fully clothed?"

"Yes."

"What did that tell you, Detective Zoren?"

"Quite obviously that she was not taking a bath when she drowned."

Several jurors snicker. Dalton ignores them and continues with his cross. "How do you know then that it wasn't an accident?"

"Well, as I stated on direct, she had numerous bruises on her body including a large one on her forehead."

"Any throw rugs on the bathroom floor?"

"Yes, one large one that was ruffed indicating to us that there had been some kind of scuffle."

"Or that she had slipped on the rug and that could have accounted for its ruffed condition?"

I watch Zoren cross his legs attempting to assume a more relaxed pose before answering, "Possible but not likely."

"So, you're discounting the possibility that Ms. Hernandez slipped on the rug while reaching for the faucet to turn off the water prior to disrobing, and in the process hit her head, tumbling into the water?"

"She also had multiple other bruising over the rest of her body."

"I see. And if she were dazed and struggling to get out of the tub with water soaked clothes and slipping and sliding, isn't it possible that could account for the other bruising?"

"Possibly, but not likely."

"If someone were trying to stage a drowning, wouldn't the killer have removed Ms. Hernandez' clothing?"

"Not necessarily."

"Oh, come now Detective Zoren, a minute ago you scoffed at the idea that the drowning might have been accidental because Ms. Hernandez was fully clothed. Isn't the inference just the opposite?"

"What do you mean?"

"Why would the killer go to all of the trouble of killing someone in that fashion when there were quicker and more efficient methods to accomplish the task?"

"I still don't understand."

Dalton goes to the front of the podium positioning himself closer to the witness. "Let me posture it this way. To perform such an elaborate scheme requires the expenditure of time. The longer the time a killer remains on the premises, the greater the likelihood of being caught in the act. Right?"

Still with a puzzled look on Zoren's face, Dalton continues, "The neighbor you mentioned in your report never indicated how long the visitors remained at the residence, did she?"

"No."

"Did the neighbor indicate whether or not either or both visitors entered the residence?"

"No. She said she returned to watching TV."

"Did she indicate how long she watched TV?"

"She stated it was approximately one hour."

"Did she state what she did next?"

"Yes, she said she looked back out the window at the senator's residence."

"Did she indicate whether the car she described with the two occupants was still at the senator's residence?"

"Yes, she stated it was no longer there."

Dalton nods. "So it's possible then that neither visitor went inside, correct?"

"That's correct."

"Isn't it also possible that after the visitors left, someone else arrived at the senator's residence while Ms. Westermeyer was still watching television and went inside and caused Ms. Hernandez' death?"

"I guess anything's possible."

"As part of your testimony on direct, you stated the evidence pointed to Ms. Hernandez being waterboarded. Did your investigation disclose what type of information was sought to be elicited?"

Zoren rubs his brow before replying, "No, that still remains a mystery."

"Along those lines, are you suggesting the defendants, the visitors described by the neighbor, waterboarded Ms. Hernandez?"

"Who else could have done it?"

Judge Goldstein interrupts, "Detective Zoren!

A witness is to answer questions, not ask them!"

"Sorry, Your Honor." Turning to Dalton, Zoren responds, "The evidence leads in that direction."

"What evidence?" Dalton persists.

"The note and ten thousand dollars."

"You mean People's Exhibit A?"

"Yes."

"Utilizing People's Exhibit A, point out to the jury, if you would, where the so-called hitmen were instructed to waterboard Ms. Hernandez."

Zoren flushes and without looking at the exhibit, replies, "There was nothing like that in the note."

"Mr. Betcher," Judge Goldstein says, "I think this would be a good place to take a recess." The judge bangs his gavel, "Be back here in fifteen minutes. Bailiff, escort the jury out."

• • •

After the recess, Dalton continues his cross-examination of Detective Zoren. "Referring your attention to the incident in the balcony of the U.S. Senate Chamber resulting in the arrest of Britt Taggert, I assume neither you nor Detective Parker were present. Correct?"

"That is correct."

"Did either you or Detective Parker review the video that was taken at the U.S. Senate?"

"Yes, we both did."

"Did it appear that either of the defendants in this case had a weapon?"

"No, not that we could tell from the video."

"Do you know what the rule is regarding weapons in the Capitol Building and the Senate Chamber in particular?"

"Only special persons are allowed to be armed."

"Such as CIA agents?"

"Yes, and certain members of the security unit."

"While reviewing the video, did you see any CIA agents that you recognized?"

"Yes, two."

"Do you know their names?"

"Yes, Eric Watson and Kenneth Samuels."

"Do you know whether they were armed?"

"I presume they were."

"Do you know what they were doing there?"

"It was part of their job. We learned later that there had been a plot to assassinate Senator Ratcliff and that the agents were there to protect the senator."

"Did there come a time when you became aware that my client, Britt Taggert, was a Virginia State Trooper and that the codefendant in this case, Megan Duval, was working for the CIA at the time of the incident at the Capitol Building?"

"Yes."

"When the defendants were interviewed at the D.C. Metropolitan Police Department, didn't both of them state the purpose of their presence?"

"Yes."

"What did they tell you?"

"Both said they were there to protect Senator Ratcliff."

Dalton thumbs through his notes. Looking thoughtful, he then asks, "Isn't it a fact that there was and is no evidence whatsoever that Britt Taggert ever had the note and ten thousand dollars in his possession?"

"Only what Chief Buchannan told us."

"Do you have any corroborating evidence to support Chief Buchannan's contention?"

"No."

"Did you ever have such evidence?"

"No."

"Thank you, detective," Dalton says and begins to gather his notes.

• • •

Judge Goldstein sits up straighter in his chair and asks, "Mr. Betcher, does that conclude your cross of this witness?"

"Yes, Your Honor," Dalton replies and walks toward the defense table.

As soon as Dalton is seated, Judge Goldstein

nods to Link. Link picks up his yellow legal pad, scoots his chair back, and stands. Once at the podium, Link organizes his notes, squares his shoulders and addresses the witness.

"Detective Zoren, you make it sound as though the critical pieces of evidence in this case are the note and the ten thousand dollars. It that a correct assumption on my part?"

"Yes."

"Thank you. Now, would it be important to know whether my client, Megan Duval, had *provided* the note and ten thousand dollars to Chief Buchannan *before* or *after* the incident at the Senate Chamber and *before* or *after* her arrest?"

"Yes, of course."

Placing his hands on either side of the podium, Link leans forward and asks, "Why would that be important?"

Zoren pauses briefly before answering. "Because if it was *prior* to the incident and Ms. Duval's arrest, it would tend to support her claim that she and Mr. Taggert were trying to foil the assassination attempt."

"Exactly! And if it was *after* the incident and after Ms. Duval's arrest, then what?"

"It would tend to show the defendants' role as hired assassins."

"And that the defendants were caught with the goods and were likely suspects in the murder of Ms. Hernandez, correct?"

"Correct."

"Would you agree the successful prosecution of the defendants hinges on who to believe?"

"What do you mean?"

"Didn't Ms. Duval indicate, when she was interviewed by the police, that after she received the note and ten thousand dollars in the mail, she tried to turn the envelope containing those items over to her boss at the CIA, Steve Cunningham?"

"Yes."

"Didn't she also indicate that, in the process of trying to solicit Cunningham's help, she learned that he was in on the assassination plot?"

"Yes."

"Didn't she also tell you and Detective Parker when she was interviewed that since she no longer had confidence in the CIA, she and Mr. Taggert, as a last resort, contacted Chief Buchannan, and informing him of the assassination plot and the existence of the note and ten thousand dollars, turned those items over to him?" Link asks and looks at the jury.

"Yes, the defendants told us that, but as I've already testified, Chief Buchannan disputes the timing and the manner in which he came into possession of the note and ten thousand dollars."

"Yes, you did state that that's what Chief Buchannan told you. However, we're trying to establish a timeframe here. You testified a moment ago that it would be important to know whether my client, Megan Duval, had *provided* the note and ten thousand dollars to Chief Buchannan *before* or *after* the incident at the Senate Chamber and *before* or *after* her arrest. Is there any dispute over the fact that Ms. Duval had the aforementioned items in her purse when she entered Chief Buchannan's office with Britt Taggert?"

"Appears she must have had them with her."

"Then how would Chief Buchannan even know she was in possession of those items if she hadn't told him about them and *produced* them for his inspection?"

Zoren looks confused and asks, "What's your point?"

"Unless Chief Buchannan is a mind reader, he wouldn't have known about those items unless he was informed of their existence by Ms. Duval and given the opportunity to inspect them. In other words, isn't it more likely then that she would have produced the items to Chief Buchannan of her own volition in order to provide proof of the assassination plot?"

Zoren, apparently realizing this is not looking good for the chief answers, "Not necessarily."

"Again, you're relying solely upon what Chief Buchannan said and discounting everything you were told by Ms. Duval and Mr. Taggert, correct?"

Shifting again in his chair, Zoren replies, "I guess you could say that."

Link looks back into the spectator section and asks, "Do you know whether Chief Buchannan was involved in the assassination plot?"

Zoren, looking shocked, sits up straighter and places his hands on the arms of the witness chair and leans forward, "Are you suggesting Chief Buchannan was part of the plot?"

Looking sternly at Zoren, Judge Goldstein says, "Detective Zoren, as I've previously stated, you're here to answer questions—not ask them!"

"Sorry, Your Honor," then to Link, Zoren says, "Could you repeat the question?"

"Yes, but let me rephrase it," Link replies. "It was only sometime after the defendants' appearance in Chief Buchannan's office that you became aware of the note and the ten thousand dollars, correct?"

"Yes."

Link studies his notes briefly then asks, "Prior to the arrest of the defendants, Chief Buchannan never mentioned the items or that the defendants had brought them in seeking help in preventing the assassination of Senator Ratcliff? Correct?"

"Yes, that appears to be the case."

"When the defendants were arrested, there's no mention in your report that the note and ten thousand dollars were taken from them, is there?"

"No."

Link then delivers the crushing blow. "Who provided the note and ten thousand dollars, if you know, to the evidence custodian at the police department?"

I watch Zoren scratch his head and look at Schumacher for a lifeline. Schumacher grimaces and shrugs as if to say, "Don't look at me for an answer." Zoren, visibly shaken, responds with another question of his own. "Are you suggesting Chief Buchannan planted the evidence?"

Judge Goldstein whips his glasses from his face, and looking even more agitated, leans toward Zoren and barks, "How many times must I warn you that it's your job to answer questions—not ask them!"

"Sorry, Your Honor," Zoren sheepishly replies and slumps down into his seat.

"Please continue," the judge says to Link.

"Thank you, Your Honor." Then looking at

Zoren, Link says, "Let me rephrase the question. The only one who claims to have taken the note and the ten thousand dollars from Ms. Duval at the time of her arrest is Chief Buchannan. Correct?"

"Yes."

"Doesn't it appear then that the statements given to you by the defendants were more plausible than Chief Buchannan's claim that he *confiscated* the envelope marked People's Exhibit A containing the note and the ten thousand dollars?"

"That's not for me to decide. That's why we have jury trials." Zoren's answer is weak and his demeanor is that of a whipped pup.

"Detective Zoren, let's talk about the so-called eye witness. Being an advisory witness, you were allowed to remain in the courtroom during Mr. Schumacher's opening statement to the jury. Is that not true?"

"Yes."

"Did you hear him outline the testimony of Irene Westermeyer?"

"I did."

"Who is Irene Westermeyer?"

"She lived across the street and was a neighbor of Senator Ratcliff."

"Did you interview Ms. Westermeyer?"

"Detective Parker and I did."

"What did she tell you?"

"It's in our reports."

"Detective, the reason I'm asking you is because the jury has not read your reports."

I watch Zoren flush with embarrassment. He finally answers, "She said she saw what looked like a man and a woman drive up the circular driveway of Senator Ratcliff's residence."

"Was she able to describe the occupants of the vehicle?"

"She said it was raining too hard to get a good look. She said the woman stayed in the car while the man ran to the door. She said he had the collar of his coat turned up apparently against the rain."

"Did she say she saw either of their faces?"

"No."

"Was she able to describe the vehicle they arrived in?"

"She said it was a dark SUV."

"Was she able to provide the make or license plate number?"

"No."

Link repositions himself and leaning one elbow on the podium, asks, "Other than the assumption that the visitors appeared to be a man and a woman, was there any forensic evidence whatsoever that either Ms. Duval or Mr. Taggert had ever been inside Senator Ratcliff's residence?"

"No."

"In fact, Detective Zoren, there's no evidence whatsoever that the visitors, or either of them, were in any way involved in Ms. Hernandez' death, is there?"

I watch Zoren squirm as he replies, "No, not really."

"Come now, Detective Zoren, you can be more definitive than that. Tell the jury what evidence you have that the visitors were in any way connected to Ms. Hernandez' death."

Looking thoughtful for a moment, Zoren finally replies, "Only that they were at Senator Ratcliff's home at about the time of Ms. Hernandez' death."

Link has done his homework. He runs rapid fire through the next questions:

"But, the woman in the car, according to Ms. Westermeyer, never left the car nor went to the door of the Ratcliff residence. Correct?"

"Correct, at least not during the time Ms. Westermeyer was watching the residence."

"And according to Ms. Westermeyer, Ms. Hernandez answered the door, which means she was alive when she spoke to the male visitor at the door. Right?"

"Yes."

"And that the so-called male visitor never entered the premises and the door was closed by Ms. Hernandez after a brief conversation with the male visitor—which means she was alive at the time the male visitor returned to his car. Is that also correct?"

Detective Zoren looks perplexed. It's obvious he's never been backed into a corner. He answers, "Yes."

"Thank you, Detective. No further questions."

Detective Parker doesn't fare any better on cross-exam by Dalton and Link. Our attorneys establish, through the testimony of the prosecution witnesses, that the note and the ten thousand dollars together with our presence in the Senate Chamber and at the senator's residence prior to the death of the senator's maid appears to be the only evidence that ties Tag and me even remotely to the murder. I'm worried that that may be all they need to return a conviction.

• • •

At the recess, Tag and I meet with our attorneys in one of the conference rooms. Link says, "Our case hinges on Buchannan's testimony. He's going to be a tough nut to crack. Without a motive for him to lie, the case may boil down to his word against yours."

"With Samuels, Harris and Crawford out of the picture," Dalton says, "the only ones who can tie Buchannan into the conspiracy are Cunningham and Watson. Now that Watson has dropped out of sight, it's damn sure Cunningham isn't about to seal his own fate by testifying against Buchannan. In fact, neither Cunningham nor Buchannan want to open up *Pandora's Box*."

• • •

When court reconvenes, the prosecution calls Westermeyer and Buchannan to the stand. Both testify as predicted. However, Westermeyer's credibility is destroyed on cross-examination by Dalton as he hammers home the witness' own statement that she was unable to clearly see the occupants of the vehicle because of the downpour. Buchannan, however, weathers the storm and comes off believable.

When the prosecution rests its case, the judge calls for a lunch break. The defense team gathers in one of the conference rooms at Dalton's law office and Dalton's secretary orders in sandwiches and drinks. As we eat, our attorneys discuss the damage inflicted by the testimonies of the prosecution witnesses. As I sit and listen, it's obvious that one doesn't have to be a genius to realize that without a miracle, our fate is all but sealed.

• • •

Once we're back in the courtroom, the defense begins its case in chief. Tag and I are called to the stand and we both reiterate our stories just as the events unfolded. The prosecution, however, is relentless in its cross-examination and it's obvious we're no match for Buchannan. Schumacher painstakingly points out in his final argument that greed was our motive and that, because we have a motive to lie and Buchannan doesn't, we must be guilty.

• • •

Even without the testimony of the three deceased key witnesses, the prosecution did a brilliant job of making us look guilty. The jury deliberates for only three hours. When they reach a verdict and are brought back into the courtroom, I can tell by the smile several jurors flash Schumacher as they enter that we're on a sinking ship.

Buchannan and Cunningham, looking smug and self-assured, are seated in the spectator section on the prosecution's side of the courtroom. They're huddled together, engaged in private conversation. Judge Goldstein has barely called the court to order for the announcement of the verdict when the double doors to the courtroom bang open, startling everyone in the process.

"It was like a western movie," a reporter would later describe the scene in the local rag. "Although there was no drum roll or puff of smoke, an unlikely figure emerged seemingly from nowhere. Every eye was riveted on a frail man as he ambled up the center aisle toward the front of the courtroom."

"Oh, my God," I say aloud to no one in particular. "It's Watson!"

• • •

Watson didn't bother with his disguise this day. He wanted Cunningham and Buchannan to know who was hammering the final nail into their coffins. During the last few weeks, his battle with cancer had diminished him and he'd lost a lot of weight. His face was so gaunt that when he entered the courthouse and walked through the metal detector, guards he had known for years didn't recognize him. This afforded him some degree of anonymity and he breathed a sigh of relief. Knowing he was a wanted man, he reasoned that if he were recognized, he'd be taken into custody and chances were he'd be dead before he could testify.

• • •

I grab Link's arm, "Link, that's Watson!"

Judge Goldstein leans forward, obviously irked by Watson's abrupt appearance.

"You, sir, are interrupting a court proceeding.

Bailiff, remove this man…"

"WAIT!" Link is instantly on his feet.

The judge now directs his attention, and obvious ire, toward Link. "Mr. Turnbull!"

"Your Honor, the man standing before you is Eric Watson, the missing prosecution witness."

The judge rears back in his chair, and taking his glasses off, says, "Is that right?" Then to Watson, he asks, "You, sir, state your name!"

"Eric Watson."

The courtroom erupts in chaos as reporters scramble for the door.

Judge Goldstein stands, and banging his gavel, shouts over the din, "This is a court of law, not a three-ring circus. You will remain in your seats until the conclusion of this hearing. Everyone, put your cellphones away or I'll have them confiscated. Bailiff, guard the door and don't let anyone leave the courtroom unless I say so."

I'm surprised by the judge's take-charge attitude. Apparently, so is everyone else. The courtroom is suddenly very still. I glance around. Cunningham and Buchannan both look pale and I see desperation in their eyes.

The judge resumes his seat and pointing to the prosecutor, says, "Mr. Schumacher, I believe Mr. Watson is *your* witness. You may proceed with direct."

"Thank you, Your Honor," Schumacher says, and his voice quivers when he speaks. Schumacher is apparently just as stunned by Watson's appearance as the rest of us.

Watson is sworn in and takes the witness' stand. Schumacher approaches the podium and it's apparent by his perplexed expression that he hasn't prepared for this witness and is flying by the seat of his pants.

"Please state your name and occupation for the record," Schumacher begins.

"Eric Watson. I'm an employee of the CIA and stationed at Langley in McLean, Virginia."

Before Schumacher can ask another question, Watson holds up a restraining hand. Looking up at the judge, Watson says "If it please the court," then he erupts into a coughing spell. "Sorry, Your Honor. I have terminal lung cancer and not much time left. My trip to the courthouse was a struggle for me physically and I don't know if I'll be able to sustain a long direct and cross." Watson's statement is interrupted several times by coughing spells, and it's apparent that he's on his last leg.

"Mr. Watson," the judge says, "what do you request of the court?"

"May I just tell my story in my own words?"

The judge looks at Schumacher. "Mr. Schumacher, any objection?"

"None. This witness is on our witness list and is called as a prosecution witness. More to the point, it's obvious Mr. Watson is in a great deal of pain, and because of the unusual circumstances, the prosecution does not object to allowing Mr. Watson to give his testimony in narrative form."

Judge Goldstein nods and then addresses Dalton and Link asking the same question. Our attorneys look at each other. After engaging in a brief quiet conversation, Link says, "No, Your Honor. The defense does not object provided we may be allowed to question the witness at the end of his testimony if need be and to object to his narrative if the circumstances warrant."

Judge Goldstein agrees to the stipulation. He then directs Watson to proceed in his own words. I'm resigned. After all what can Watson say that can make things look worse for us?

"Thank you, Your Honor," Watson says and begins. The courtroom is dead silent. We sit and listen as Watson takes us through the ordeal from beginning to end. His narration is often interrupted with violent coughing spells.

When Watson identifies Buchannan and Cunningham as the kingpins who orchestrated the assassination of Senator Ratcliff, Cunningham stands and shouts, "You lying bastard! I did no such thing!"

Judge Goldstein jumps up, and with rage written on his face he shakes his fist at Cunningham ordering him to sit down and be quiet. Cunningham slumps back into his seat.

Watson, unabashed by the outburst, continues. He confesses that he and Samuels killed Jessica Stanton and Marcella Hernandez. Then, as if to add insult to injury, he points a finger at Cunningham and identifies him as the person who gave the orders.

The judge glares in Cunningham's direction obviously daring him to disobey his previous order to sit and remain silent. Cunningham, apparently fearful of being held in contempt, says nothing.

Watson states that the hit was not only on Senator Ratcliff but Tag and me as well. He vividly describes how he and Samuels followed me from place to place with the intent to kill me and retrieve the envelope. He also testifies that he personally knew that Buchannan and Cunningham had invested a considerable amount of money in crude oil futures and stood to lose a fortune if the proposed coal phase-out bill was passed in the Senate—thus establishing that elusive motive the prosecution kept mentioning that Buchannan didn't have and therefore had no reason to lie.

Watson is visibly drained at the conclusion of his narrative. He bends forward and dissolves in a violent coughing fit.

"Mr. Watson," Judge Goldstein says, "are you finished testifying?"

Unable to verbally respond, Watson nods his head.

"Let the record reflect the witness has concluded his testimony," the judge says to the court reporter. The judge now asks our attorneys if they wish to cross-examine the witness. They both say no.

The courtroom is as quiet as a church. Both the prosecution and the defense sit in stunned silence watching Watson seal the fate of Buchannan and Cunningham, and in the process, exonerate Tag and me.

Judge Goldstein clears his throat. "Because of the new testimony introduced into evidence, I'm sending the jury back to consider Mr. Watson's testimony in arriving at a verdict." When the jury is dismissed, I watch Buchannan and Cunningham stand and move toward the exit. Judge Goldstein must have also noticed their attempted exodus. He banged his gavel loud enough to wake the dead and shouted, "Stop those two men!" pointing his gavel at Buchannan and Cunningham. The deputies assigned to the courtroom jump into action and immediately take the pair into custody.

"Take your hands off of me," Cunningham shouts at one of the deputies. "Who in the hell do you think you are?"

The judge stands again, and in a restrained voice, shouts, "They're seekers of truth and justice—that's more than I can say for you." The judge then wraps his robe around himself, sits down and orders the deputies, "Get them outta here!"

• • •

It was barely thirty minutes before the jury returns with not guilty verdicts. Armed with the newly discovered evidence, the jury no doubt was transferred from *Hang the Bastards to Pin a Medal on the Patriots* (Tag and me). But then again, we were never advised of what the original verdicts were.

PICKPOCKET — JUDITH BLEVINS & CARROLL MULTZ

CHAPTER NINE

Peek-a-Boo...

After our cases are disposed of, Tag and I are returned to the detention facility to complete the release process. As we wait in one of the interview rooms for the property custodian to conduct an inventory of our personal belongings and return them to us, I'm experiencing a variety of feelings. Frustration and disgust top the list, however, they're intermingled with the relief that we were vindicated without having to present our case; anger that we were even charged in the first place; gratitude that Watson did the right thing by coming forward and confessing; and sadness that so many lost their lives to benefit a few greedy men— just to mention a few.

Tag elbows me interrupting my musings. I look up. Through a window in the door, we watch as Nate Buchannan and Steve Cunningham are escorted into the booking area by several deputies. From our vantage point, it looks as though the two of them are engaged in a violent argument. The scene is so intense, I suspect, if they weren't handcuffed they would have come to blows.

Remembering all the horrific situations the two of them put us through, I feel no sympathy for them, only contempt. Tag reaches across the table and takes my hand, I smile at him. "Looks like the chickens have finally come home to roost," he says.

"You don't think they'll pull some strings and…" I ask, genuinely concerned the nightmare may not be over.

"After the hostility Judge Goldstein demonstrated toward them after Watson's testimony, I don't think their tentacles reach far enough to get them off this time. Goldstein will most likely not be appointed to hear their cases. Their attorneys can, and probably will, scream judicial prejudice in the unlikely event Goldstein is appointed."

Tag has been my savior throughout this whole ordeal and I feel safe with him close. His words are comforting. "What's going to happen to them?" I ask.

Glancing back at the melodrama unfolding in the area beyond our tiny room, Tag says, "They'll go through the same legal process we just went through." Tag's eyes darken as he adds, "Don't judge the tree by the one, or in this case two, bad apples. Law enforcement, for the most part, consists of decent, loyal and honorable individuals."

I squeeze his hand, "I know, I found one."

Tag squeezes back.

Still watching Cunningham and Buchannan

being booked, I say, "From the looks of things, they may turn on each other before they even get to trial."

Tag laughs. "You're very insightful. If I were in their shoes, especially with an eyewitness of Watson's caliber, I'd be first in line to ask to see the DA ASAP to cut a deal."

"Think they can both get a deal?"

"Depends on who sings the sweetest. This situation is a prosecutor's dream. They could both plead guilty and possibly get some sentence consideration. In the process, the DA rids society of two sharks without breaking a sweat."

"Your words paint a vivid picture. That's what I call just desserts! Perhaps a clever warden will assign them the same prison cell and they can be roommates for the next fifty years."

Tag tosses his head back and emits a hardy laugh. "My, my! You have a mean streak I didn't know about," he teases. "And I love it!"

After a brief pause, I ask, "What's going to happen to Watson?"

"Probably not much—at least not in this lifetime. Doctors apparently give him less than a month He'll be held at the detention facility in the infirmary until..." Tag pauses for a moment, then continues, "I'm sure, under the circumstances, the

DA will immediately video tape his deposition incriminating Cunningham and Buchannan. Also, his testimony during our trial fingering Cunningham and Buchannan for orchestrating the murder of Marcella Hernandez and your friend Jessie will be used against those swine if they decide to go to trial."

• • •

The door suddenly swings open and one of the deputies enters. He hands each of us a manila envelope, "Here 'ya go. As soon as you verify all your personal property has been returned to you, you're free to leave." He hands each of us a release form and a pen. "Sign the form when you're ready…"

Tag dumps the contents of his envelope out on the table and sorts through them. "Looks good," he says, and signs the form handing it back to the deputy.

My envelope contains the contents of my purse and a small gold cross necklace. I sign the form and hand it back to the deputy not taking the time to examine the contents.

"You're now free to leave," the deputy says as he stores the signed forms in a file folder. "When you're ready, I'll escort you to the door."

• • •

When we leave the detention facility and step out onto the sidewalk, freedom for me takes on a whole new dimension. The air I breathe is fresher, the sky above is bluer, the song birds' chirping is sweeter, the grass in the park across the way is greener, even the roar of the passing traffic is music to my ears. I slip my arm through Tag's and squeeze him close to me. He slips his arm around my waist. Life is good.

"Where to, Tiger?" he asks.

"Anywhere," I reply, "as long as it's with you…"

"Hum…that could be dangerous," he says with a smile.

"If you recall, I'm the one who got us into all this mess."

"Yes, now that you mention it, I do recall how you suckered me in." After a brief pause, he adds, "Besides, being unpredictable is part of your charm."

When I look up at him, the glint in his eye says it all. *I think the boy's in love with me.*
Before I can respond, he says, "Look, Meg! There's an empty park bench, let's sit for a while and enjoy our new found freedom."

Sitting in the park across from the detention facility somehow doesn't appeal to me at the moment. "Perhaps we could…"

"Ah, come on, humor me," Tag says and takes my arm guiding me through the park toward the bench. Once we're seated, he wraps his arm around my shoulders and scoots close to me. "I was thinking," he begins, "remember when we talked about taking a slow boat to China?"

"HA! Do I ever. I believe that was right before we were arrested and dragged through the quagmire…"

"Right. And do you remember me saying 'Tell ya what, Tiger, when we get the bad guys behind bars, we'll take that slow boat to China on our honeymoon and you can experience the Orient firsthand."

My chin drops. *Is he proposing?* "I… I…"

Without missing a beat, Tag says, "I'll take that as a yes." He then reaches into his breast pocket and pulls out a colorful paper cigar band and places it on my left hand ring finger. "I just happened to come upon this unique little treasure during my recent tour of the county jail," he says, twisting the band around my finger. "It's almost one of a kind and I'll let you keep it if you'll say you'll marry me…."

"I… I…"

Again, without missing a beat, he says, "I'll take that as a yes," and pulls me into an embrace.

"Wait!" I say and push him back. "There's

something you should know before I commit."

"What's that?" he asks, his voice laced with disappointment.

"I have another love I'm obligated to."

I watch his face fall, "Okay, go on," he says and takes a deep breath.

I take Tag's hand in mine, "You see, he saved my life and I owe 'em."

"Un-huh," Tag pulls his hand out of my grasp. "So, does that mean there's no you and me?"

"NO, no. Not at all. In fact, after you and I are married, I'd like for him to come live with us."

Tag jumps up and facing me places his hands on his hips in a defiant manner. "Not on my watch! With me it's all or nothing…I'm going to be *the* man in your life, not *a* man in your life."

I've not seen the jealous side of Tag and I suppress a smile. "Settle down!" I say, and pat the bench beside me encouraging him to sit. "You may not be so opposed when you hear my story."

"Don't count on it!" he grumbles, and plops down next to me. He folds his arms across his chest tenaciously hanging on to his defiance. "I'm listening…go on."

I sense he's at the exploding point, and not wanting to exacerbate the situation, I launch into my encounter with Moochy, the cat at MickyD's, and how Moochy saved my life that day. I'm relieved when I see Tag start to relax. I continue telling him how Watson and Samuels followed the garbage truck making it possible for me to make my getaway. At the conclusion of my rendition, Tag bends over roaring with laughter. A few moments later he's still snickering as he wipes tears from his eyes. "I'd be honored to have Moochy move in with us."

I throw my arms around his neck and embrace him, "Thank you, I knew you'd understand."

"Hell! I love cats…"

"You do?" I pause for a moment then ask in a pleading voice, "Think he's still there?"

"One way to find out. Come on," Tag remarks. Standing he takes my hand and pulls me up from the bench.

We exit the park and take a taxi to Tag's apartment. Going inside, we take a quick look-around and determine his residence is just as he left it. When we were incarcerated, Chris Monahan, a friend and fellow state patrolman offered to keep an eye on Tag's place and take care of his vehicle. Thanks to Chris, both are in pristine condition.

• • •

It's late afternoon when we arrive at MickyD's. I eagerly scan the parking lot when we enter and am disappointed when I don't see Moochy. Tag pulls into a parking slot and we walk to one of the umbrella tables on the patio.

I call out, "Here, kitty, kitty!" Still no sign of Moochy.

"I think maybe we need something to entice him, like a sausage McMuffin," Tag says, and heads for the entrance.

I nod and watch him enter the restaurant. When Tag rejoins me, he unwraps a muffin, breaks it apart and places the pieces at our feet under the table. A few moments into our wait I sense something under the table. Looking down I see the yellow ball of fur, he's rubbing against our legs.

"There you are, you little dickens," I exclaim and gently pick him up. He purrs and rubs his whiskers against my face. He then squirms loose from my grasp, and jumping down, he attacks the muffin.

Tag leans over and peers under the table. "Guess you know what his first love is," he teases.

EPILOGUE

The year's lease on my apartment is about to expire, and since Tag's place is in a better location and much larger than mine, we decide to keep his and let mine go. Moochy has already been set up in Tag's laundry room with the cat-necessities and he appears to be very comfortable in his new digs.

When Tag was exonerated by the court on all charges, he was reinstated by the state patrol and today is his first day back on the job. I'm still waiting to hear about my job at the CIA. The director interviewed me and told me the agency would review my case. It appears that my having prior knowledge of Jess' illegal activities and not reporting them may be held against me.

At the interview, after explaining to me the agency's position, the director asked me if I wished to make a statement in my behalf. Reliving that conversation, I now mull over my account of the events and wonder if I could have stated my involuntary involvement more effectively.

I remember saying, "Yes, sir, I would like to explain how I became embroiled in this mess," I began, hoping to minimize the consequences regarding my job.

"You may. Go ahead."

"Thank you, sir. You see, Jess and I were roommates during our four years at Wellington-York. In fact, we were as close as sisters. It was during our junior year that Jess confessed to me that she was a pickpocket and that's how she managed to survive."

The director raised his brows but said nothing.

Not knowing how to interpret his silence, I rushed on. "After graduation, we found jobs and had separate lives. During the ensuing five years we kept in touch. Although we had a standing weekly luncheon date, our relationship changed and the subject of her illegal activities never came up again until…"

I paused as I watched the director jot down something on a note pad. *Am I painting myself into a corner?* I fidgeted feeling unsure of myself—and weighed every word I said.

"Go on," the director urged.

"It was at lunch. I think it may have been the day after she picked the wrong pocket, that she appeared to be overwrought and anxious. She told me about lifting an envelope and what it contained and asked me to talk to Steve…"

"Steve?"

"Yes. Former Special Agent Steve Cunningham…"

"Ah, yes, that Steve. Go on," he urged.

"Jess pleaded with me to get some advice from Steve regarding what to do with the envelope. Her anxiety was mainly over having taken so much money and how to rectify it. Usually, her take would be under a hundred dollars. Most victims, she said, wouldn't go to extremes to recover a small amount. I'm pretty sure Jess hadn't found the note—she would have said something if she had."

The director continued taking notes and I remember shifting in my chair wondering if I'd disclosed too much. Anyway, it was too late so I continued, "Jess and I agreed that going to the police was out of the question because she would be arrested and probably lose her job. She said she hoped Steve could come up with a solution."

"I see. And did you contact him?" the director asked, looking up at me.

"No. I argued that it may not be a good idea to involve Steve but told her I'd think about it." I felt tears forming in my eyes and dabbed at them with my fingertips. This part of my narrative was very emotional for me, and suppressing my urge to cry, I continued, "The next and last time I heard from her was when she called the night she was murdered asking me to meet her at her place.

"Jess sounded desperate so I rushed to her

apartment. That was when I found her body. That very night I began the fight of my life." I remember pausing and taking deep breaths to calm down as I vividly recalled how my life changed.

The director nodded.

"I believe the subsequent events are outlined in the police reports forwarded to your office…" I said.

"Yes. We received the detailed reports from the D.C. Metropolitan Police Department," he replied.

I held my breath. The director looked thoughtful and after a few moments, stood and came around his desk. Taking my hand and helping me from my chair, he said, "Ms. Duval, we're in the process of conducting our own investigation and if our findings validate your story, I don't see any reason to terminate your employment. Your involvement was obviously not of your own choosing." He walked me to the door and opened it, "You'll be hearing from us within the next few days."

"Thank you for giving me the opportunity to explain," I said, as I stepped out into the corridor. "I understand the agency's position."

I loved my job and dreaded the thought of losing it. As I leave the building, I become melancholy thinking this may be the last time.

It's late afternoon and the sun is setting;

twilight is rapidly approaching. When I leave the CIA facility, I go directly to my apartment. I haven't been back there since the night I fled after Jess was murdered. I open the door and step into the foyer and a musty, stale odor assaults me, probably from the place having been unoccupied for several months. Advancing into the living room, I look around and the once comfortable surroundings now seem foreign to me—too many ghosts are lurking in the shadows. I try the light switch but the electricity must already have been turned off.

The last rays of the afternoon sun highlight a photograph on the fireplace. It's a photograph of Jess and me in our caps and gowns on graduation day. I walk over and carefully wipe the dust from the two smiling faces with my shirt sleeve. I'm suddenly overcome with sadness. Being in these familiar surroundings triggers the memories of those dreadful days, and because of the roller coaster I found myself on, I'd not had a chance to grieve over the loss of Jess. It suddenly hits me and I completely break down. After a few minutes I regain my composure and swipe tears from my cheeks. I head for the bedroom. *I'm not going to let them ruin even one more minute of my life.*

Other than an accumulation of dust, my bedroom looks the same as it did the night I left.

During the last couple of months I was clad either in my navy blue Walmart uniform or my orange jail garb. I'd almost forgotten what it was like to have more than one change of clothes. When I swing my closet doors open and see my clothes hanging there, it's like Christmas and I squeal with delight. Although none of the garments in my collection are of the Neiman Marcus variety, my wardrobe now looks like a million bucks. I pull on my favorite jeans and a soft, warm T-shirt. *Now, that's more like it!*

The sun finally slips below the horizon and it's beginning to get dark. The gloom is frightening—I see something scary lurking in every corner. Inspired by fright, I work as fast as I can packing my clothes and other personal items. I cram everything I own into my two remaining pieces of luggage and maneuver them to the front door. As I pass through my small apartment I check each room to ensure I haven't overlooked any of my belongings.

Satisfied I've done a thorough job, I don't look back when I close and lock the door behind me. When I reach the lobby, I stop to say goodbye to Jimmy, the doorman, and leave him my keys.

"Going to miss you, Ms. Duval," Jimmy says as he places the keys in a desk drawer. He walks me out of the building and helps me load my luggage into my car.

"I'm going to miss you, too, Jimmy," I say and give him an affectionate hug before I slip onto the driver's seat. He closes the car door, and as I drive away, I look in the rearview mirror. Jimmy's standing on the curb waiving at me. Still looking in the rearview, I notice a dark sedan pull up beside Jimmy. I'm stopped at a traffic light so I continue to watch. I see the lone occupant of the sedan lean over to the passenger side window and say something to Jimmy. When Jimmy points my direction, the hair on the back of my neck begins to tingle.

Remembering how I felt in the semi-dark apartment, I chastise myself for being so paranoid. *Stop it, Meg! You're seeing something sinister everywhere you look. After all, the bad guys are locked up... Still...*

The light changes, and as I proceed through the intersection, I keep an eye on my rearview mirror. I don't see the sedan following me, so I relax a little.

• • •

Tag's still at work when I arrive at his place. I park in the parking garage and take the elevator to the third floor. Wheeling my luggage into the bedroom, I begin to unpack. As I do so, I notice my clothing smells stale from not having been laundered for several months. I pick up a load and take it to the laundry room.

When I open the door, I almost step on Moochy who is laying spread eagle on his back adjacent to the laundry room doorway. He apparently chooses to ignore my presence as he contentedly snoozes away when I enter. I step around him to get to the appliances. Plopping my load down, I sort the whites into the washer and start the water. Just as I'm about to add a cup of bleach to the mix, I sense someone behind me. I stand paralyzed.

"Just stay where you are…" the intruder orders.

"Who…who are you?" I stutter, staring straight ahead. Afraid to move I stand rigid, still holding the bleach suspended above the washer.

"Me? I'm the equalizer!" the intruder says and punctuates his comment with a sinister laugh. "It's 'cause of you, Ricco don't trust me no more. I'm an outcast among my peers…"

I take a chance and turn my head slightly. From the corner of my eye I see him start to move forward. Still watching, I notice that he apparently hasn't spotted Moochy who is still partially blocking the doorway. As the intruder steps into the laundry room, his foot lands square on Moochy's tail.

"MEOW!" Moochy screeches and jumps up onto the dryer.

I seize the opportunity, and taking advantage of

the distraction, I turn and throw the cup of bleach into the intruder's face.

"MY EYES, MY EYES!" he shouts and drops his gun. He falls to his knees and begins to rub his eyes with his clinched fists.

Wasting no time, I grab Moochy and spring out of the laundry room headed for the front door. Tag must have just come in. He grabs my arm as I whiz past, stopping me midstride. "Meg, what is it! Are you all right?"

Although I'm relieved to see Tag, I'm so traumatized I'm unable to speak. I point to the laundry room. Tag nods and pulls his service weapon from his holster and shoves me behind him. "You stay here," he orders and begins to move cautiously toward the rear of the apartment. We can hear the intruder moaning.

I have Moochy in a tight grip under my arm and follow close behind. As Tag creeps along, he swishes at me with his free hand trying to encourage me to stay put. There's no way I'm going to let him go it alone. I violently shake my head so Tag finally relents.

When we reach the laundry room, the intruder is curled up in a fetal position with his face clasped in his hands. "What happened to him?" Tag asks.

"I…I threw bleach in his face."

Tag looks at me, "Quick thinking!" he says. He then kneels beside the man and picks up the gun lying on the floor next to the intruder. Placing him in handcuffs, Tag pulls the intruder up into a sitting position, and says to me, "Get some cool water in a bowl and a cloth."

When I return, Tag begins to bathe the intruder's eyes. "Who are you and what are you doing here?" he asks.

"My name is Tony."

"Tony what?" Tag demands.

"Tony Basselli."

"And what in hell's name are you doing here?"

"I came to even the score," Basselli says.

"What score? What are you talking about? I've never seen you before in my life."

Basselli throws me a contemptuous look. "Her! She ruined my life. I had it pretty good until they…"

"They?"

"Yeah, her and that damn pickpocket…"

I sag against the doorway. *Is this nightmare ever going to end?*

Tag drops the cloth into the bowl and looks up at me. Then to the intruder, he says, "Okay, you've said enough. Save the rest for the police."

• • •

It was almost two weeks before I hear from the CIA about my employment. In part, the letter reads:

...Because of the nature of our organization, we seek to employ individuals who are independent thinkers and able to respond to adverse situations on a moment's notice. Your conduct during the attempted assassination of Senator Ratcliff was exemplary. Having put your life on the line to save the Senator's was above and beyond your paygrade. It is therefore the opinion of this board that you are a credit to the CIA and we are fortunate to have you in our employ...

I refold the letter and put it back in the envelope. Tag looks at me, "Well?" he asks.

"Well," I say with a broad smile, "our founding fathers would be proud of me."

• • •

As the criminal prosecutions against Tony, Ricco, Buchannan and Cunningham progressed, we followed the events with morbid curiosity. The media had a heyday playing up the "corruption at the highest level" theory. It was like a game of Dominos. Tony rolled over on Ricco; Ricco rolled over on Buchannan; Buchannan rolled over on

Cunningham and before long there wasn't anybody left to roll over on. All the bad guys ended up behind bars.

• • •

Tag and I have a simple wedding with a few friends in attendance. Fortunately, several months before the wedding Tag had substituted the cigar band with a diamond engagement ring. After champagne toasts and the ceremonious cutting of the wedding cake, Tag pulls me aside and surprises me with a delightful wedding present.

"I'm a man of my word," he says, and hands me an envelope.

"What's this?" I ask, turning the envelope over and inspecting it. There's no clue on the outside as to what it contains.

"It's your wedding present—from me and Mooch."

Not knowing what to expect, the suspense mounts and my hands shake as I peel the flap open on the envelope. I carefully pull out the contents and squeal when I see what Tag's surprise is—two tickets for a week's cruise aboard the *China Doll*. Still clutching the envelope in my hand, I wrap my arms around Tag's neck and hug him tightly.

"I take it you're pleased," Tag croaks, and gently pulls my arms away from his neck.

"I am indeed," I say, "but what about…"

"It's taken care of," Tag says. "Chris offered to cat-sit in our absence."

• • •

It's our last night aboard ship, and standing at the rail watching the moon rise over the China Sea, Tag asks, "Did you have fun?"

I hug Tag's arm closer to my body as a soft breeze embraces us. Gazing off into the distance, as we watch the moon's reflection being rippled by the motion of the ocean, I reply, "Absolutely! I'll never forget this trip. China is so intriguing—it's everything I imagined it would be and more." Tag slips his arm around my waist.

"Wonder how Moochy's doing," I muse.

"A better question is wonder how Chris is doing?" Tag teases.

"Now, now," I say. "After all Moochy saved my life—twice!"

"So that means you only have seven left?"

"I think the nine lives myth only applies to cats."

"Okay, whatever," Tags says. Then drawing me closer to him, he continues, "Just promise me, in the future, you'll refrain from testing the theory."

I flinch when Tag says "promise" and instinctively cross my fingers remembering my childhood ritual whenever I made a promise I wasn't sure I could keep. However, this time the commitment feels different and so do I.

"I promise," I whisper, and standing on my tiptoes, I uncross my fingers and seal my promise with a kiss.